DRAGON WARS

WIZARD WATCH

BOOK 8

CRAIG HALLORAN

DON'T FORGET YOUR FREE BOOKS

Join my newsletter and receive three magnificent stories from my bestselling series for FREE!

Not to mention that you'll have direct access to my collection of over 80 books, including audiobooks and boxsets. FREE and .99 cents giveaways galore!

Sign up here!

WWW.DRAGONWARSBOOKS.COM

Finally, please leave a review of WIZARD WATCH-Book 8 when you finish. I've typed my fingers to the bone writing it and your reviews are a huge help!

WIZARD WATCH REVIEW LINK! THANKS!

Dragon Wars: Wizard Watch - Book 8

By Craig Halloran

★★★★

Copyright © 2019 by Craig Halloran

Amazon Edition

TWO-TEN BOOK PRESS

PO Box 4215, Charleston, WV 25364

ISBN eBook: 978-1-946218-80-3

ISBN Paperback: 979-8-629204-24-4

ISBN Hardback: 978-1-946218-81-0

WWW.DRAGONWARSBOOKS.COM

Publisher's Note

This book is a work of fiction. Names, characters, places, and incidents either are the product of the author's imagination or are used fictitiously, and any resemblance to actual persons, living or dead, events, or locales is entirely coincidental.

❋ Created with Vellum

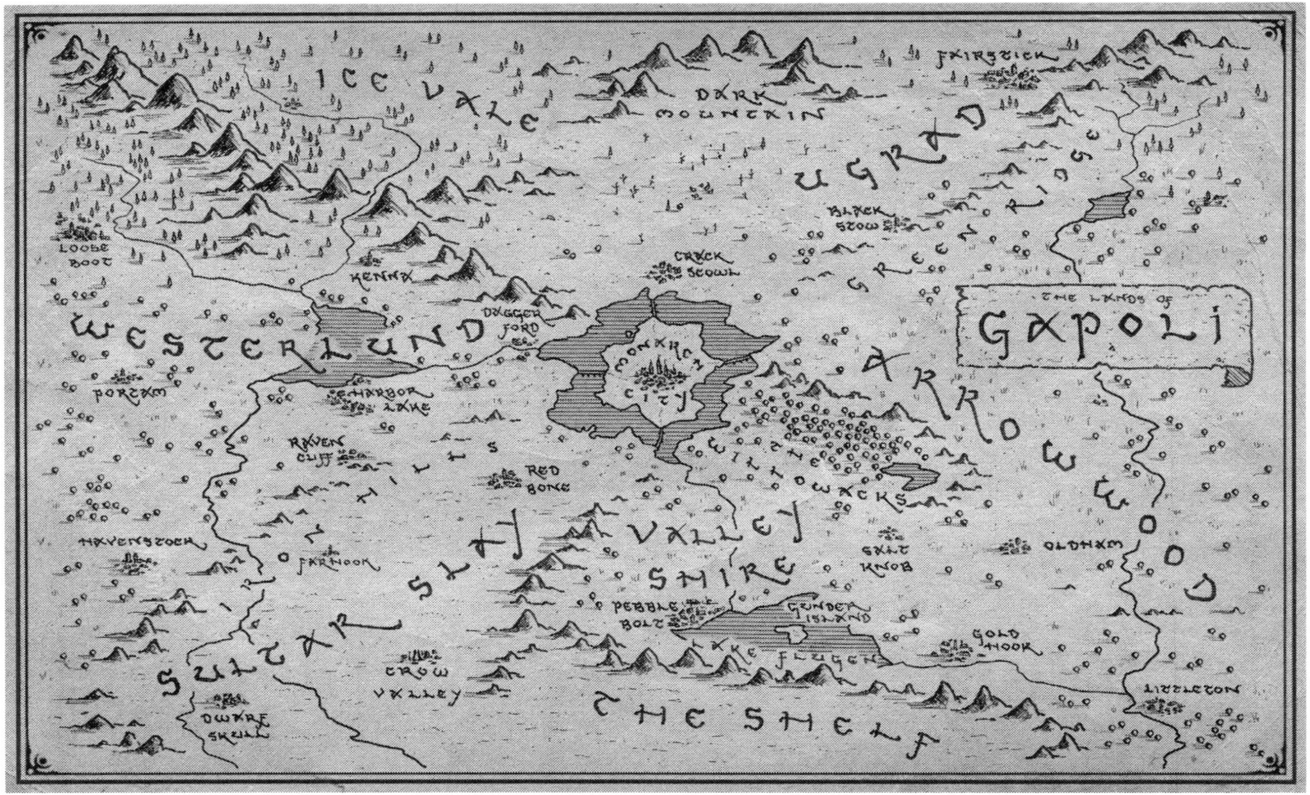

THE LANDS OF

GARDOR

ARROWWOOD

COTTONWOOD

LITTLETON

OXFIELD

FAIRFIELD

DARK MOUNTAIN

PITKEN WOODS

WILLOWCKS

HOOK

JAGGED TOOTH

BOOK CITY

THE SHELF

ICE VALE

CRACK

DRAGGER FORD

HENRIK

DRAGON LAKE

RAVEN CLIFF

RED BONE

CRAGS VALLEY

DWARF SKULL

WESTERLUND

FORLORN

DARKMOOR

NEVERSTORM

LOOSE BOOT

WIZARD WATCH: ARROWWOOD

Talon had made camp near the Wizard Watch tower in a grove of yellow elm trees that were peppered with burning-orange leaves. The leaves fell like soft rain with the off-and-on breezes. An orange leaf from the midsize trees fell on top of Razor's face. With his eyes closed, the handsome young warrior brushed it away and rolled to one side.

Zora smirked at Reginald the Razor curled up like a child with his face to her campfire. It was midday, chilly, and she warmed her fingers over the flames. It had been three days since Grey Cloak, Dyphestive, Tatiana, and Streak had entered the tower. There hadn't been contact with them since.

She stirred a stick in the fire's coals.

Where are they? Zora glanced over her shoulder. She

could see the ominous tower through the branches and shivered. *I hope they're fine. No, they have to be. Don't be wrong. You have to trust Tatiana.*

Needless to say, the atmosphere outside the tower had been nothing short of prickly. She'd been left alone with Razor, Thanadiliditis, Leena, and the frosty Anya ever since. She and Anya weren't speaking. It didn't help that Leena didn't speak either.

At the moment, though cold, things were peaceful in the camp. Anya and Than were hunting. Leena was gathering wood, leaving Razor and Zora alone. It didn't take long to realize that Razor was decent company. He was cocky but good, young, too, somewhere between her age and Grey Cloak's, but he acted like he had the knowledge of a fifty-year-old. All of them did.

"If you keep those eyebrows knitted too long, they'll stick together," Razor said in his charming but rugged voice. He'd caught her staring into the flames, fingering the Scarf of Shadows.

She turned her attention to him. "Is it that bad?"

"Most people worry." Razor rubbed his mouth, stretched his arms out over the grass, and yawned. He sat up. "But I don't worry. Worry creates doubt. Doubt will get you killed." He braced himself against the tree behind him. "I sound like I know all, but I don't."

"It's fine. I'm getting used to hearing that from everyone else, especially you know who."

Razor glanced at the surrounding woodland. "Ah, you're talking about Fiery Red, aren't you? Heh. She's really something, that gal." He nodded his strong chin. "I like her, though. She's up-front about things. And she's a dragon rider. They're an aloof kind, as I understand. Elite. A woman with a dragon is a good woman to have... they say."

"She doesn't have a dragon, just dragon breath."

Razor waved his hand with a growing smile. "Whooo, it's getting hot out here."

"You know what I mean." Zora was squatting and tucked her hands into her sides. "She's mean."

"I can handle that meanness when she's that pretty."

"Are you that shallow?"

"Heh, I like her. She's a fighter, like me. You have to be mean to survive. You've been around the dungeon. You know that."

Zora gave him a straight-faced look. "I thought you were Tatiana's man."

"I wish, but she's in love with a ghost. Don't get me wrong, Zora. I trust Tatiana, too, but I don't fault Fiery Red for mistrusting her." He pulled his dagger out of his sheath and spun it in his hand with a flashy motion. "Fighters like us put our faith in flesh, bone, and steel. Those wizardly things are beyond us. Besides, she's got great hair." The fingers on his free hand grazed his short, feathery brown locks. "Like me."

Zora rolled her eyes but didn't hide her smile. Razor was pleasant to listen to, rough but positive.

Leena appeared out of the woodland and dropped a handful of broken branches by the fire. She sank to her knees and started building a spit from some of the sticks she'd carried.

Zora and Razor exchanged amused glances.

Leena did everything with determination and purpose. Her silky black robes with gold trim contrasted sharply with her long cherry-red hair, which was braided into a tail behind her head. Her long fingers with black nails were quick and dexterous as she bound the sticks together with small vines that she used like twine. Leena caught Zora looking at her and stuck her expressionless face out toward Zora.

Zora looked away.

Razor giggled. "I think someone is missing someone."

Zora couldn't help herself. She addressed Leena. "Do you want to talk about it?"

Leena glared at her.

Razor burst into raucous laughter.

The contagious hilarity had Zora bursting into tears as she clamped her hands over her gut. She fell to one side. "It's not supposed to be that funny. Sorry, Leena."

Leena tilted her head to one side, eyes studying Zora like she'd lost her mind. She removed her nunchakus.

"Bwah-hah-haaa-hah!" Razor fought to spit his words

out. "She's going—going to throttle you with her little s-s-s-sticks!"

With tears streaming down her cheeks, Zora rolled flat on her back, laughing her head off. She couldn't contain it. She looked at Leena. "I'm sorry. It's not you, Leena. It's—it's those cute little sticks! Ah-hahahahahah!"

"Stop it. You're going to make me pee my trousers!" Razor said.

Leena suddenly stood up, and her brows knitted together. She wasn't looking at Zora, however. She was looking in the direction of the shadow that had fallen over her.

Razor's laughter was cut short.

Zora's sputtering fell flat as well as she cast her eyes on Anya.

2

Anya carried a dead young stag over her shoulders. Sweat beaded on her face, and the edge of her wavy red hair was damp. With a thrust of her legs and a heave of her shoulders, she dropped the stag to the ground. "He's young, but his rack has six points," Anya said as she pulled out her dagger and took a knee by the carcass. "So, have Grey Cloak and Dyphestive returned? I don't see them."

Zora ground her teeth.

"Not yet," a wide-eyed Razor said as he climbed to his feet. "You caught that stag? No simple feat, especially with full armor."

Than glided out from between two trees with a smile on his old wrinkly face. "She crept up on it and slew it before it blinked," he said in a scratchy voice. "It was something to behold." Even though Than was older and walked with a slight stoop, the long-haired hermit stood taller than the rest of them.

Using her blade like a hunting knife, Anya cut deep into the stag's belly. "Ah, there's the heart. You should eat that, Zora. It will make you strong... and wise."

Zora's face soured as her belly churned. She'd seen Adanadel and Browning carve up plenty of deer back in the day, but she'd never developed a stomach for it. Tanlin hadn't either. She crept back.

Anya slung a hunk of meat at her. "Don't gawk. Cook. Aren't you hungry?"

"Do you have to be so arrogant?" Zora tried to pick up the slab of meat with a stick.

Leena bent over, snatched up the bloody meat, stuck it on a pointed stick, and took it to the fire.

Anya continued to saw. "Arrogant? That's not a very nice thing to say to the person who brought enough food for you to eat over the next several days. I assume it'll be several days or forever."

"You don't have to stay!" Zora shouted. Her head throbbed, and her heart beat in her temples.

"Look whose nostrils are flaring," Anya said in an annoyed but cool manner. "I'll wait it out. It's worth it to let you know that I'm right."

Than moved between the two women. "There's no need to bicker. We're all on the same side of the battle. You need to remember that."

Zora moved to the other side of the fire, drumming her nimble fingers on her dagger. "Everything was fine until she showed up." She moved deeper into the woodland and sat down under a tree. *I hate her.* From a distance, she watched the others grab a hunk of meat and start to eat.

Razor gushed about the stag. "It's so tender. If we can eat like this, I don't care if we wait for weeks."

It was all Zora could stand. She covered her ears and put her head between her knees.

Since Grey Cloak and Dyphestive had left, it'd taken everything she had to hold herself together. She missed them, and with each passing hour, she carried more doubt about Tatiana. The elven sorceress could be as frigid as Anya, and Zora had no doubt she carried secrets very close to her chest.

I've never felt so alone. Perhaps I should go home, back to Raven Cliff. I miss Tanlin.

It wouldn't have been so bad if Crane and Jakoby were still along. They were easy to talk to, especially Crane. He had a story about everything and had seen so many places.

Than approached. He had a small steaming hunk of meat on the end of a stick. He sat down by Zora and offered it to her. "Please eat."

"I'm not hungry."

"Come now, I heard your belly growl. Eat." He nodded at the campfire. "In spite of Anya."

"Huh." Zora took the stick, peeled off a piece, and

chewed on it. The warm meat was very tender. She took another bite off the stick.

"Good, eh?" he asked.

She shrugged. "Could be better." Her eyes lingered on his scaly arms, which looked like shedding snakeskin. His fingernails were sharp and long. She hadn't had many conversations with Than. "Are you a leper?"

Than chuckled. "No. I'm only old and getting weaker by the day." His low voice carried a soothing tone. "They're actually scales."

She lifted a brow. "Does everyone in your world have scales?"

"No, mostly the dragons. It's a long story." He combed his fingers through his stringy red-gray hair. "Very long."

"So, is your world like this one?"

"Very much, or at least it was until Black Frost started to drain it."

"And you've been to other worlds as well?"

Than nodded. "A few."

She sighed. "I wish I could go to another world."

Than put a gentle hand on her shoulder. "There's no place like home. Believe me. And don't let Anya spoil things for you. She's not against you. If she were, you'd be dead."

"That's comforting."

"She's an ally. Believe me."

"Says the hermit from another world."

A moment passed before he added, "I'm a very good judge of character. You're in good company."

She turned toward Than. "What about Tatiana? Do you trust her?"

"She has a good heart, but I fear that she is being deceived." He looked off in the direction of the Wizard Watch. "Tatiana has placed a great deal of faith in the mages in the towers. It's what she knows. We can only hope that she can see the truth for herself before it's too late."

"You don't trust the Wizard Watch either?"

"I know little about them. That's a good reason not to trust them."

Zora chewed the rest of her meat and tossed the stick away. "Thanks. Tell Dirty Red it was wonderful. I think I'll take a nap." Just as she turned her back to Than, she caught a soft white glow out of the corner of her eye. Someone entered the camp. "Dalsay!" She popped up from her spot and rushed over.

Dalsay stood by the fire in a full but ghostly form that she could see right through. He was still in his dark-blue robes, with a head of long, thick brown hair and a beard. His fingers with many rings were clasped together. "I have news," Dalsay said.

"Spit it out, apparition," Anya demanded.

Dalsay nodded. "Grey Cloak and Dyphestive are gone."

3

Anya's dragon blade sliced right through the ghost of Dalsay. "Die, cretin liar!"

"Even your dragon steel cannot harm me," Dalsay said calmly. "And I'm not here to bear ill will. They are safe, only gone, as I understand it."

"We'll see if my blade will cut you or not!" Anya's dragon sword shone blue with dancing fire. The very metal hummed and crackled. She thrust.

Dalsay vanished and reappeared twenty feet away underneath a great oak adjacent to the camp. "I came to tell you to depart north to the elven city of Staatus. Reunite with Crane there and await further instructions."

Anya let out an animallike growl and charged Dalsay. He vanished a split second before she thrust her sword into the heart of the tree. The blade sank halfway to its hilt. She tugged on the steel, which held fast in the tree. Her face filled with strain.

"Need a hand?" Razor offered.

Anya shot him a dangerous look. "Stifle it!" She planted the bottom of her boot against the tree's bark and put her shoulders into it. "Eeeeyargggh!"

The sword came free.

Anya's chest heaved underneath her breastplate, and her nostrils flared. "I told you this would happen," she said to Zora. "You never should have trusted that witch!"

"Me?" Zora practically spit when she said it. "I didn't tell them to come here or go in there. They made that decision. Did you ever think that they did it to get away from you?"

Anya's emerald eyes burned like fire. She stormed off in the direction of the tower.

Everyone followed, including Zora.

Anya's right! Tatiana, what did you do to me? Where are you?

Than caught up with Anya. "Where are you going?"

"In there," Anya said without so much as a glance at the tower, but everyone knew what she was talking about.

Anya started hacking into the thorns and bristles towering over the group like a woman gone mad. Her blade ignited with blue fire.

"She's gone plum crazy," Razor uttered under his breath.

Hunks of the thistles burned with new flames. More of the dry wood caught fire as Anya mowed into it like a bull. The path widened as she pressed through the brush, the thorns scraping against her armor. She made it through, but the fiery gap started to close.

"Come on!" Zora said. She raced through the closing thorns.

Razor was the last one through before the thornbush sealed them inside the grounds surrounding the tower.

Anya's face was scraped and bleeding from forehead to chin. That didn't stop her from marching toward the tower. She stomped around the perimeter of it. "Where's the door, you bloody cowards? Where is it?"

All the tower walls were flawless, without the seam of a single door in sight. Even Zora's keen eye picked up nothing.

Anya found a spot on the white granite stone that looked like an archway that had been sealed up long ago. Using her blade, she chopped into it. Chips of stone flew, but the damage was minimal.

Zora stepped back from the tower and looked up. The architecture was brilliant, with separate levels of stone columns encircling it. It stood several stories tall, and the top jutted into the sky like a finger pointing at the passing clouds.

"He said they aren't there," Zora said loudly.

Anya stopped swinging her steel and looked at Zora like she was a fool. "And you believe him?"

Zora felt like an idiot. She'd trusted Tatiana and Dalsay faithfully for years, but when it came to it, she'd started to doubt. She clenched her jaw. *Dirty acorns. She's right.* "I'll climb."

Anya gave her a dirty look. "What?"

"I said I'll climb." She searched for a handhold. "In the meantime, the pair of you can keep trying to chop this tower down. Let's see who gets inside first." Her fingers found purchase on the rough stone of the columns at the bottom, and she started to climb. "See you on the other side."

She'd made it up the first ten feet when she noticed that Leena had joined her. The monk from the Ministry of Hoods crawled the column like a bug and was gaining ground.

"Impressive." Zora sped up her efforts, climbing like a squirrel to the next level.

Down below twenty feet, she saw Razor, Than, and Anya watching her. Anya's hair covered one eye. With her sword in hand, she stood frowning.

"What's the matter? Did you chip your sword?"

Razor hollered up with his hands cupped around his mouth, "Be careful, Zora!"

"Thank you, swordsman obvious! Gah!" She had looked up to see Leena standing on the narrow ledge right beside her. "Don't spook me." She tilted her head. "You go that way. I'll go this way. Look for any opening we can squeeze through."

Level after level, they made their way toward the top. The tower was sealed up as tight as a drum, with only the smallest cracks and creases between the stones. A platform about ten feet wide with a capstone made of steel sat at the top.

Zora took a seat with her feet dangling over the rim. A stiff wind rustled her hair and clothing, and the chill froze her fingers. She blew hot breath into her hand as Leena joined her. "Well, this was a waste."

Whether Leena was hot or cold, one could never tell. Her face remained without expression. All the monk did was lift her fingers and point to a flock of great birds coming their way.

"Great, they're probably going to poop on us," Zora muttered.

Leena shook her head.

"What?" Zora narrowed her keen eyes. The birds didn't have feathers. They had scales. "Horseshoes!"

4

Z ora cupped her hands over her mouth and shouted downward, "Anya! We're going to have company! Dragons!"

It wasn't the first time she'd seen dragons in the sky. It wouldn't have been the worst thing, either, if not for the fact that the dragons were flying right at them instead of passing overhead.

"We need to get down. We don't stand a chance up here," she said to Leena.

Leena jumped off the ledge.

"Leena!" Zora cried out. The monk was down on the next level of the tower. Her fingers gripped the columns. She glanced at Zora and dropped down again.

"How in the world is she doing that?" With a glance

over her shoulder, Zora saw the dragons bearing down on her.

The dragons were small, like ponies, with long faces covered in hard, bumpy ridges and putrid-green eyes. They opened their jaws wide and screeched like birds of prey.

She eyed the ground, where Anya, Razor, and Than were waiting. Leena was halfway down. "Here goes," she said and jumped as a dragon sailed right over her head.

Zora's fingers skidded against the round column. Her toes hit the rim of the outer ledge and slipped off. She caught hold of the same ledge with the tips of her fingers and held on for her life. Her feet dangled over the ledge as another dragon soared by. "Not good!" She wouldn't make it to the bottom in time without falling or the dragons getting her first. She swung herself onto the tower's balcony and nestled her body behind a column.

Another dragon soared by and let out an earsplitting screech. A fourth followed.

Zora pressed her body deeper into the space behind the column. Her heart pounded in her chest. Her breathing quickened, and her limbs froze.

Again, a terrifying screech blasted through the air. A dragon rose before her from below and fixed its serpentine eyes on her. The dragon landed on the ledge with its wings beating behind its back. It steadied and came at her.

She opened her mouth but couldn't make a sound. Fear took over her mind. Silently she screamed, *Noooooooo!*

ANYA'S EYES locked on the thunder of dragons soaring through the sky. She raised her sword and sneered. "Those aren't dragons. They're drakes."

"Ah, the foul ones," Than added.

"If Cinder were here, he'd tear them to ribbons. They're the vermin of the skies." Anya waved her arms over her head and shouted, "Come, winged lizards! Come and let me introduce you to death."

Leena hopped down the last ten feet of the tower and landed like a cat. Her nunchakus were spinning in her hands. She fixed her eyes on the drakes and joined her companions.

"There's a dozen of them," Than said as he picked up a branch. "Their arrival is very peculiar."

"It's the work of wizards, if you ask me." Anya set her feet in a defensive stance and eyeballed the dragons.

A foursome of the drakes set their eyes upon her and dove.

"Incoming," Than commented quietly.

"Good," she said.

"Time to carve some turkey," Razor added.

The drakes landed and surrounded the small company. They spread their wings wide and hemmed the group in.

Unlike dragons, the drakes had small talons on the

ends of their wings. Their bodies were supported by powerful back legs that launched them into the sky, but they didn't breathe fire. Their long tails had spikes on the end and were used for strangling and striking.

"Careful, Leena. They're stupid but very nasty," Anya warned. "Don't let them get their claws on you, or they'll tear you in two." The drake nearest Anya coiled its long neck back and struck with its head. Anya lunged at its face. Her sword skewered its mouth shut. She twisted and wrenched the blade free.

The wounded drake's screech could have shattered glass as it backed away. It wriggled its neck violently. Its eyes burned with primordial hate as it came at Anya again.

Anya set her feet, put her hips into her swing, and let loose.

Slice!

The drake's head came clean off, putting its threatening shrieks to an end.

RAZOR CHARGED with his swords thrust forward. The drake collided with him, horns lowered. Steel clashed with horn as the drake plowed him over. The foul creature sank its teeth into the leather armor and meat of Razor's shoulder. Its back claws raked over his legs, trying to rip him apart.

Overpowered by the savage reptile, Razor let go of his long blades and whisked out the smaller ones. "I won't die on my back." Using the daggers like pointed fists, he punched into the drake's abdomen again and again.

THAN WRESTLED WITH ANOTHER DRAKE. The large hermit had the drake in a headlock. It tried to shake him free. Incredibly, Than held on. "Hold still and die, won't you? I haven't broken a neck in a long time!"

LEENA'S NUNCHAKUS SPUN FURIOUSLY. She busted the drake in the snout six times before it could attack.

Clok! Clok! Clok! Clok! Clok! Clok!

She jumped over its tail, hopped onto its spiny back, and unleashed another torrent of glowing nunchaku power.

Clok! Clok! Clok! Clok! Clok!

The drake's skull cracked underneath the hammering blows. Its body sagged and flattened on the ground, trembling.

Leena jumped from its scaly hide. Her taut muscles eased as she scanned her surroundings. She didn't see the drake's death strike coming. Its spiked tail lashed out and struck her in the belly. Leena sagged.

Anya rushed to her aid and chopped off the drake's tail. She caught Leena in one arm as the speechless woman fell. "Hang on, Leena. Hang on."

Leena's eyes rolled up into her head, and her eyelids closed.

5

"Don't die on me, Leena," Anya said. Blood from Leena's belly stained her hand as she tried to put pressure on the wound. "Be strong."

She heard a loud snap, like a branch breaking.

A drake died in Than's arms. He shoved the dead drake away. Panting for breath, he joined Anya. "I don't think they're after us." He pointed at the tower. "They're after her."

The rest of the drakes nestled on different levels of the tower, crowding around the last spot where they had seen Zora. Their wings fluttered as they sat on their perches, and they let out nauseating shrieks.

"We need to save Zora," he said.

"What about Leena? Can you help her?"

Than placed his scaly fingers on Leena's chest. "Her

heartbeat is faint yet strong." He tilted his head. "Very strange." He pulled the nunchakus from Leena's death grip. "I don't know what good these will do, but we need to lure the drakes down here. I'll take a crack at it. Be ready."

Anya rested Leena's limp body on the ground and stood. "I'm always ready. Let it fly."

Than hurled one pair of nunchakus. The small sticks sailed end over end like the blades of a buzz saw and cracked a drake in the back right behind the wings.

The drake's head twisted around. It set its fiendish eyes on Than and shrieked. A trio of drakes jumped from the tower and dove right at them.

Than awkwardly flipped the other set of nunchakus around. "Could you spare a dagger? I'm not accustomed to using sticks."

Anya offered him both of hers. "Have at it, hermit."

As soon as the drakes hit the ground, the battle was on. The drakes lashed out with their tails and teeth. Anya gored one in the belly and hacked into the hide of another.

Than moved like an old panther and pierced a drake behind the wings. He cried out, "Aaaargh!" as the drake chomped down on his forearm. It backed up, pulling him across the ground.

Than planted his feet, sat up, and with a fierce grimace, he jammed a dagger into the top of the drake's skull. "That's good steel." Wheezing, he pulled the blade free.

Anya finished off the last drake with a hard chop into its body.

"Duck!" Than called out.

A drake flew at Anya's back and flattened her to the ground. A second drake came out of nowhere and bit her leg. Her armor saved her leg from getting bitten clean off, but the pressure built like a vise.

"Get off me, drake!" She punched it in the snout.

Another drake landed right beside her. Its tail lashed out and coiled around her neck. Together, the drakes pulled her in opposite directions. They were pulling her apart.

Through clenched teeth, with her face turning purple, she said, "Nasty things..." Anya choked as the pressure on her neck built, making her eyes bulge. Her head felt like it was going to explode. She hacked at the drake fastened to her leg. Her sword swings had a bad angle, and they had no force behind them.

Lords of the Air! They are killing me!

Out of the corner of her eye, she saw Than coming her way. His eyes blazed like burning gold. He opened up his mouth, and a geyser of bright yellow-orange flames spewed out.

Than's dragon breath ate up the drake with its tail coiled around Anya's neck. Its scales shrank to the bone, and it died in its own burning flesh.

The wroth heat of Than's air curled the tips of Anya's

hair, making it stink. The flames caught the drake's gaze. It released her and pounced at Than.

With a single gust of breath, Than turned the drake into a living pillar of flame. Its wings beat frantically as it burned to a crisp, staggered on wobbly legs, crackled a shriek, and stumbled over dead.

Two more drakes dropped from the tower. Without hesitating, Than burned them to a crisp.

Anya limped toward Than, who huffed out a ring of black smoke, and said with a raised brow, "Where did that come from?"

Than thumped his chest with his fist. "It must have been something I ate." His legs became noodles. He broke out in a cold sweat and fell down flat on his back.

"Than!"

ZORA COWERED behind the column as a drake clawed and nipped at her. She was wedged far enough back that its long snout couldn't reach her. Its small taloned hand on the end of its wing clawed at her. A talon caught her shoulder and ripped her clothing and skin. She cried out, "Augh!"

The slash from the drake woke her from her fear-filled slumber. She'd become numb to the attack, unable to move or think as the flying reptilian terror rattled her sharp mind. All she wanted to do was run, but she had nowhere to run or hide.

A second drake moved to the other side of the column. They had her pinned in behind the pillars. Their winged claws stretched out, raking at her body. Both drakes let out mind-jarring shrieks.

She covered her ears and squeezed her eyes shut. "Help me. Somebody, help me, pleaaaassse!"

6

Drake claws raked at her flesh.

"Skrrreeeeeeee! Skreeeeeeeeee! Skreeeee—"

Thuk!

Zora's eyelids snapped open.

One of the drakes had an arrow sticking out of the side of its head. It teetered on the ledge, turned, and launched itself into the sky.

Thuk! Thuk!

Two black-feathered arrows embedded themselves in the drake's chest. It flung its wings back and beat them once more before it dropped like a stone.

The last drake turned its attention to the danger coming from below. An arrow blasted into its neck. A second arrow struck it square in the chest, and it fell from the tower and smashed into the ground.

Zora crawled away from her hiding spot and looked down. She trembled. Burning drake corpses made black smoke and an awful stink. Than and Leena lay on the ground as if dead. Anya tended to them. Zora scanned the woodland edge but saw no sign of archers.

Where are they?

She envisioned several East River elves coming to their aid, but none could be found. A subtle movement caught her eye. An elf stepped out from the trees with a bow in hand. His hair was long and as dark as raven feathers, and his bare arms were strong and mighty.

Zora's heart leaped. "Bowbreaker!"

As soon as Zora's feet touched the ground, she ran and leaped into Bowbreaker's arms.

The stoic elven archer gave her a rigid hug and patted her back. "You're safe now, Zora."

Tears streamed from the corners of her eyes. "You won't believe how glad I am to see you. I thought I was dead."

"You're wounded," Bowbreaker replied in a firm voice as he eyed the nasty gashes on her arms and legs. "Let me tend to you."

When she got her first look at the blood on her arms, she almost fainted. Suddenly, the wounds burned like fire. "Please, please do."

Anya approached and squatted beside her. "You're very brave. I'm glad to see you survived."

"You are?" Zora asked.

"I would've missed having someone to fight with," Anya said coolly.

"I don't think you'd ever have trouble with that." She glanced behind Anya. "Are they...?"

"Dead? No. Than passed out after breathing fire all over the drakes," Anya said.

Shocked, Zora replied, "He's a fire-breathing hermit?"

"I wouldn't have believed it if I hadn't seen it for myself." Anya's nose crinkled. "The stink might kill us all, however."

Bowbreaker dumped water out of a leather waterskin and into his hands and washed Zora's wounds.

Zora sucked air through her teeth. She couldn't stop shivering. "I'm sorry. You must think me a coward."

"Of course not," Bowbreaker said with a handsome, creaseless expression. "There are few people in the world who could have survived the feat you attempted." He smoothed a hand down her face. "You have a brave heart, Zora."

"Uh... thank you."

Bowbreaker finished treating her wounds with green leaves and a white salve he carried in one of his packs. "This will hold you together for now. In the meantime, don't fight any more drakes."

"I'm not sure about this one," Anya said to Bowbreaker about Leena. "She took a shot in the gut."

"Excuse me." He moved from Zora to Leena and

opened Leena's robes. "It's not grave and appears to be healing on its own."

Leena's eyelids snapped open. She saw Bowbreaker and slapped him in the face.

"Apparently you're right." Anya smirked.

Leena closed her robes and sat straight up without wincing. She stared at Bowbreaker for the longest time then put her finger in front of his face, wagged it back and forth, and stood. She moved toward Than and ripped her nunchakus from his fingers. She then wandered off to find the other pair.

Bowbreaker combed his hair behind his pointed ears. "Who is that?"

"Leena. A monk from the Ministry of Hoods. I know little about her," Zora said. "She doesn't speak."

"A rare and admirable quality," Bowbreaker said in a well-mannered voice.

Was that a joke? Zora thought.

One of the dead drakes moved.

In a flash of motion, Bowbreaker was on a knee with his bow ready and an arrow nocked.

Anya's weapons were poised and ready.

The drake rolled over onto its wings, and a bloody man emerged from underneath. "What happened? Did you forget about me?" It was Razor, wounded from head to toe. He looked like he'd been eaten alive and spit back out. "How about some water?"

"SKREEEEEEEEEEEEEEYYAAAAAHHH!"

Everyone lifted their gazes skyward. A lone drake circled above the Wizard Watch tower. It wasn't like the rest of the brood. It was bigger, by three or four times at least.

"What is that?" Zora muttered.

"A firedrake," Anya said sternly. "Very dangerous. It makes the rest of the drakes look like puppies."

Razor finished crawling out from under the pile of dead drake flesh. He stood, using one sword as a cane. "Firedrake as in it can breathe fire?"

At that movement, the firedrake huffed out a mouthful of flames. Its body was armored with rigid scales. It had claws like great scissors. It was a beast, an angry beast with demonic eyes that burned with hungry hatred.

Zora felt the wroth heat from above on her cheeks.

"Tell me steel can pierce its hide," Razor said.

"Sometimes." Anya nodded as her eyes followed the creature's skyward path. She took a deep breath, and her sword started to glow again.

Bowbreaker aimed his bow.

Leena joined them with both pairs of her nunchakus in hand.

Zora summoned her strength and stood with them. "Well, if you've seen one drake, you've seen them all. Let's kill it."

The firedrake dove.

Bowbreaker let loose his first arrow. It skipped off the field of small horns protecting the firedrake's skull.

Every one of Zora's senses told her to run, but she didn't. She stood her ground, facing the fiery winged doom that was about to plow her over with the others.

7

Anya ground her heels into the dirt. She would strike to take the dragon down before it plowed her over. One perfect strike was all it would take. She concentrated. *I must be perfect.*

The firedrake dropped out of the sky halfway between them and the tower. It pulled up, its wings beating hard, and sucked in a mighty breath.

"Thunderbolts!" she said. "It's not going to attack. It's going to scorch us. Everyone, scatter!"

"You don't have to tell me twice!" Razor darted away from the tower.

A torrent of flames erupted from the firedrake's mouth. The dragon breath blasted into the ground where the company once stood. The flames turned the grass to ashes and scorched the earth black instantly.

Bowbreaker loosed another arrow. The shaft sailed true and jabbed into the firedrake's left eye.

It let out a roar that shook the branches on the trees. Wroth heat blasted out of its mouth in a cone of fire, sweeping in all directions.

Anya dove behind one of the glowing quartz stones that jutted up out of the ground. Fire blasted around her on both sides. "Everyone, scatter! Scatter! Its breath won't last forever!"

"How long will it last?" Razor shouted from somewhere unseen.

"I don't know. Hide!" she said. The firedrakes and drakes were notorious predators that would not give up the hunt until their prey was dead. As for the firedrake's breath, as far as she knew, it could set the entire forest on fire. "Take cover somewhere! I'll handle the drake!"

Anya peeked around the stone after the flames stopped. The firedrake landed on the ground. Its head hung low, and its nostrils flared. Patches of flames burned like campfires in the field before it. It let out another gust of fire, setting the thornbushes ablaze. The flames spread quickly. Suddenly, it locked its eyes on Than lying still in the field of fire. It approached him and opened its jaws wide.

"No!" Anya was on her feet and running at the firedrake at full speed.

The firedrake swung its head around on its long

serpentine neck. Its eyes narrowed, and flames spit from its mouth.

Anya covered the gap with long strides. Flames or no flames, she wasn't going to turn back. She ran on a collision course for the inferno.

"Anya, no!" Razor cried out. His words were suffocated by the roar of the flames.

Through the searing heat, Anya kept running.

Whump! Crack!

"Roooooooaaaaaaaar!"

The flames evaporated instantly.

A tail swiped Anya out of harm's way. She rolled across the ground and came back up to one knee.

Two titans were intertwined in ferocious battle. The firedrake fought for its very life against a behemoth of a dragon that had landed on top of it.

"Cinder!" Anya shouted.

Cinder dwarfed the firedrake. More than double its size, the powerful Cinder crushed the firedrake into the ground with his front paws. The firedrake blasted fire into Cinder's huge horned face. Cinder shrugged the flames off like the wind. The firedrake's back claws scraped against the armored scales of Cinder's underbelly.

Cinder pinned the firedrake down and bit into its neck. His jaws clamped down like a huge vise. The firedrake's narrowed eyes bulged. The steel-hard bones in the firedrake's neck gave way under the unyielding pressure of Cinder's jaws.

Crack-snap!

The firedrake's taut neck went limp. The fire in its eyes cooled.

Cinder slung the firedrake aside like a rag and sent it flying into the tower's walls. He sat up on his hind legs and let out a roar so loud that it scattered every bird in leagues of the valley. He was mighty, beautiful, covered in scales, hard ridges, and horns, flecked with tortoiseshell patterns of yellow and gold.

Anya ran right at him. "Sssssh! Sssssssh! You bloated bigmouth!" she said with glee. "You can't let the others hear you!" She grabbed onto his big face when he lowered his head. She hugged him tight. "What are you doing here?"

"I missed you," Cinder said sincerely.

"What about the fledglings?" She was speaking of the twelve baby dragons they had saved from Hidemark.

"They're safe. They grow fast." Cinder eyeballed her with his golden eye. "They need attention. Mentors, Anya. You need to come. Did you find Grey Cloak?"

"Yes."

Cinder scanned the others in the company, who came forward with wide eyes. "No need to fear. I'm on your side and quite friendly. Hmm... where is Grey Cloak?"

"In the tower," Anya said dryly. "They've been locked in there for days."

"They?" Cinder asked.

"Grey Cloak, Streak, and Dyphestive."

"I see."

Her lip curled. "The wizards lied to us again. They led them inside and came out and said they were no longer there. I don't believe them. The moment we tried to find a way into the tower, the drakes came." She shook her fist at the tower. "They're liars."

Cinder nodded in a manner that was more human than dragon. If anything, he came across as a wise grandfather. He scratched his chin with his claws. "You can't find an entrance."

"No," she said.

"Hmm... perhaps there's something I can do about that."

8

Cinder spent the better part of an hour using his head and horns like a battering ram, trying to bust the tower walls down.

While Leena stitched up Razor's wounds, Razor said to Cinder, "Watching you is giving me a skull ache. What are those walls made of? Iron?"

"If they were made of iron, I would melt it, but it's stone, hence it won't burn," Cinder replied. "A very clever design by the Wizard Watch, a design to keep dragons out. I fear that I cannot penetrate it. It's not the stone so much as the enchantment."

Zora noticed that whenever Cinder rammed the tower, the surrounding quartz stones glowed. "It's the rocks, isn't it?" She was standing by a pink crystalized cluster of rocks that jutted out of the earth like limestone.

"Most likely," Cinder replied. "Anya, we should return to the fledglings. They need you. They need me."

"I know." She frowned.

"Ugh…" Than fought his way to his elbows. He blinked several times, and his eyes found Cinder. "Hello."

"Hello to you," Cinder replied.

Before anyone could say anything, Than and Cinder were immersed in deep conversation, but it wasn't in any language that Zora understood. She crept over to Anya. "What are they saying?"

Anya had her arms crossed and shared the same perplexed look. It carried in her voice too. "I have no idea. I've never heard it before."

"It's beautiful, whatever it is," Zora said. "It's almost like singing."

Everyone sat down and watched the dragon and hermit talk to one another like a pair of old friends. Even Bowbreaker joined the captivated audience and sat beside Zora. She leaned into his shoulder.

The old hermit, Than, stood before Cinder with his stringy hair hanging down over his shoulders. Frequently he combed his long fingernails through what once might have been fiery-red locks. One shoulder was slumped, and he appeared weaker than he had earlier in the day, but he spoke with a new spring of energy.

Cinder appeared equally enthused. The magnificent beast's great wings flexed out from time to time as they spoke in enchanting gibberish. Cinder seemed to hang on Than's every word. He chortled gleefully from time to time. The conversation was long, and it could have gone on forever had Anya not interrupted well over an hour later.

"Excuse me!" she said on her approach. She stood between them. "I have to ask, what are you talking about?"

"Oh, we aren't talking. We're merely making our initial introductions," Than said.

Flabbergasted, Anya said, "What? All this time and you haven't been saying anything?"

"Well, we've said quite a bit, but our language contains a lot more syllables and song than yours," Cinder said. "It's been so long since I've used it. I thought I might have forgotten the words. We don't use it so much anymore, though, occasionally"—sadness filled his voice—"Firestok and I did."

Zora's knees were pulled up to her chest, and with big green eyes, she asked, "What language is it?"

"Dragonese," Than replied. "Would you like to learn it? I could teach you, but it might take a decade or two."

"We don't have time for that," Anya said, pushing Than away from Cinder. "We need to get to Grey Cloak. Now."

"Why did Grey Cloak go in the tower in the first place?" Cinder asked.

Anya sighed. "Per Tatiana's ceaseless urgings, he went in to find out what's become of the dragon charms that they've been recovering for years. Apparently, the dragon charms have not been relinquished, to the side of good, that is. I suspect they've been giving them to Black Frost all along."

"You don't know that," Zora argued.

"No, but it makes sense. Doesn't it?" Anya fired back. "Look at what happened the moment we tried to enter the tower." She pointed at the dead firedrake. "Those vermin came. Servants of Black Frost." She turned to Cinder. "You must go."

"We must go," Cinder replied.

"I'm not leaving without Grey Cloak. We need him," she said. "We need Streak too. He's a controller."

Cinder perked up. "My boy is a controller? Hah! I knew he had something special in him. However, I have twelve others to feed, Anya. We need you."

Than spoke in Dragonese to Cinder.

"Not this again," Anya said. "Make it short." She started to wander away when Zora caught her by the elbow. She gave the blond half elf a deadly look.

Zora released her. "You seem very committed to Grey Cloak. Why is that?"

"Because he is one of the last Sky Riders like me. We can't fight Black Frost without riders."

"It sounds to me like you want to stay with us," Zora said.

"Hardly, I can do it on my own." Anya searched the

others' weary eyes. "I would think that you'd be tired of my company."

"That's an understatement, but we all want the same thing. To find our friends," Zora said.

"Hah, you don't even know where to start. If they aren't in the tower, where are they?" Anya asked.

"I can't answer that, but I know who can." Zora brimmed with excitement. "Crane can find him."

"How's that?"

"The same way he found Grey Cloak before, using the Medallion of Location."

Cinder cleared his throat. "Anya, can I speak with you?"

With a wary eye, the Sky Rider approached her dragon. "Yes."

"Thanadiliditis and I have come up with an arrangement that should suffice," Cinder said.

Anya raised a brow. "And what might that be?"

"Than can return with me in your stead. He can take part in preparing the dragons," he said.

She eyed Than. The old man didn't look so well, and she could hear a faint wheezing rattling inside his chest. "What makes you think he can train a dragon?"

Than ambled forward. The gold fleck in his eyes sparkled with inner fire. "You saw me," he said in a raspy voice. "I am a dragon." His eyes searched hers. "I speak truth that I am weakening. We would all be better served if

I helped out elsewhere, but only with your permission, Anya."

She looked up at Cinder. "And you trust him?"

Cinder lowered his head. "I do, and I trust you to find Grey Cloak, Dyphestive, and my son, Streak. You can do this, Anya, but you can't do it alone. Only holler if you need me."

She kissed his cheek and said with an aching heart, "I will. Be careful, my best friend."

Than climbed into Cinder's saddle and made himself at home. A broad smile broke out on his face.

"Are you ready to ride the sky?" Cinder asked Than.

"It's been too long." He pumped his fist in the air and shouted, "Dragon! Dragon!"

Cinder launched into the sky. The thunder of his wings created a fierce wind. They darted straight for the clouds and were gone.

Zora felt for Anya. Clearly the woman was emotional, as Zora watched the fiery woman wipe a tear from the corner of her eye.

Anya turned and found everyone staring at her. "What are you looking at? Quit gawking. Onward to Statuus."

9

WIZARD WATCH

A fountain made from the whitest stone was the centerpiece of the bottom floor of the Wizard Watch tower. At the top, four huge goldfish spit streams of clear water into the wide basin below. Inside the basin were coins of all sorts, numbering in the thousands, residing below the goldfish that swam above them.

Grey Cloak paced around the fountain while Dyphestive sat on the edge with his fingers in the water. Streak swam among the fish, gobbling them up on occasion. His tail suddenly flipped out and splashed Dyphestive.

"Streak, what are you doing in there?" Dyphestive asked as he wiped the water from his face. "Will you get out of there? You've eaten enough fish already."

Lost in his own world, Grey Cloak didn't pay them any

mind. He was too busy studying his strange surroundings. The four walls were over twenty feet high and formed a perfect square, unlike the smooth cylinder of the tower. Each wall had a beautiful archway made of the purest obsidian that shone against the bronze lanterns burning with an enchanted flame of sunlight. More dancing lights, like stars in the sky, illuminated the space above their heads.

Behind each mural was a grand painting of different locations all over Gapoli. One mural showed the towers of Monarch Castle from a distance. Another painting was an aerial view of the burning black volcanoes surrounding Dark Mountain. Many places Grey Cloak had never seen before. A few he had. The paintings slowly shifted and changed from one landscape to another.

At one point, he saw Portham in the far west, and for a moment, he longed for the meager life he'd had on Rhonna's farm. *I wonder how the old crow is doing without us to boss about.*

"Dyphestive, how long have we been here?" he asked.

"I don't know." Dyphestive scratched underneath his tawny locks above his ear. "A few hours."

"Hmm... I can't tell if the moments pass like hours or the hours pass like moments."

Dyphestive looked above him. "It's difficult when you can't see the sky. I'm sure Tatiana will return soon."

"Yes, of course. She's so reliable." Grey Cloak moseyed away from the fountain and closer to the murals. The entire time they had been inside, he'd yet to see another person. Aside from the burbling waters in the beautiful fountain, the expansive room was very quiet and serene. "Do you remember which way she left when she went?"

Dyphestive had a befuddled look as his eyes swept the room. He pointed at the mural in front of him. "She walked that way and vanished into a picture of fields."

"What sort of fields?"

"A pasture of grass, rather."

"Funny, that's not how I remember it. I seem to recall her walking up a flight of steps to a magnificent castle, like Monarch City." He shook his head as he ran his fingers over the painting on the stone wall. The paintings were solid but still moving. "I fear she might have duped us again. Zooks." He raised his voice. "Tatiana, where are you?" His voice echoed once before getting drowned out by the cascading waters.

"Streak!" Dyphestive cried out.

Grey Cloak turned on his heel. "What is it now?"

"He splashed me again."

"You could move," Grey Cloak said.

"I don't want to move. I like watching the fish, but Streak keeps chasing that one and making me wet." Dyphestive reached into the waters. "Get out of there, Streak. You've had enough fish!"

It wasn't like Dyphestive to lose his cool. The brawny youth was even-keeled most of the time. Grey Cloak ambled over to see what was going on.

The fountain's basin was a ring twenty yards wide and at least two feet deep. Goldfish of all colors filled a third of it. Streak knifed through the waters with his tail slithering underneath, propelling him forward.

"Do you see that one?" Dyphestive poked his finger at the water "The big silver one." There was excitement in his voice. "Streak is chasing it, but it's much too quick, even though it's bigger than the other fish."

Grey Cloak fixed his gaze on the silver fish. "I bet I could catch it."

"Huh, even you aren't that quick. Trust me. I've been watching that fish. It's like a hummingbird in water," Dyphestive commented.

"I'll wager that I can."

Dyphestive turned and looked at his blood brother. "I'll wager that you can't. What do you want to wager?"

Grey Cloak sawed his index finger over his chin. "The next time we capture treasure, I'll take your share or you can take mine."

"You never gave me my entire share the last time."

"Of course I did." Grey Cloak removed his boots. Balancing on one foot at a time, he took them both off with ease, revealing his bare feet. He wiggled his toes. "Heh, it's been a while since I've seen you."

Dyphestive pinched his nose. "And smelled them."

"Ha ha." Grey Cloak extended his hand. "Bet?"

Dyphestive took his brother's hand in his crushing grip. "Bet."

10

G rey Cloak waded through the knee-deep fountain waters and hovered over the silver fish. Unlike the fist-sized goldfish, which were spotted with white, gold, and black scales in some cases, the silver fish was the biggest fish of all.

The silver fish was as long as Grey Cloak's arm from wrist to elbow. It had the long whiskers of a catfish and large snow-white eyes. Its small fins flapped and waved in a steady, hypnotic pattern.

I have you, Grey Cloak thought. His trousers were rolled up over his knees, and he squatted deeper into the water. He slipped his hands underneath the clear water and eased them closer to the silver fish. *You're mine.* His hands made a cradle around the fish's body. He grasped at it.

The silver fish squirted away from his fingertips like it

had been shot out of a crossbow. It blazed a stream of silver to the other side of the pond.

Grey Cloak slapped the water. "Thunderbolts! That's one fast fish!"

Dyphestive chuckled. He sat on the rim of the fountain with both of his bare feet in the water. "You've been going at this for over an hour. Let me take a stab at it."

"Is that a joke?" Grey Cloak asked.

"No. Just because you can't catch it doesn't mean that I can't."

Grey Cloak jabbed a finger at Dyphestive. "We still have a bet."

"I know." Dyphestive slid his broad frame into the water. "How about this? Whoever catches the fish first wins?"

Grey Cloak considered it and rubbed his chin. "You're on!" He charged through the fountain, splashing water everywhere. Stretching the distance between him and Dyphestive, he scattered the schools of goldfish and dove at the silver fish.

Once again, the silver fish squirted away without him even getting close.

"Zooks!" he hollered.

"I see it!" Dyphestive jumped at the silver fish. It darted right underneath him as he belly flopped into the water. He popped up, soaked from head to toe, and slung his hair out of his eyes. "Horseshoes, that fish is fast! It's like a dart."

Streak swam by Grey Cloak's feet on a path toward the silver fish.

"Oh, no you don't! You aren't getting in on this too," Grey Cloak said. He grabbed his dragon by the tip of the tail and hauled him out of the water. He held Streak out upside down at arm's length. "This is between me and Dyphestive." He wagged his finger at the dragon. "You stay out of this."

Streak shook his bull neck.

"You heard me, Streak," Grey Cloak warned.

The runt dragon huffed out a mouthful of inky smoke. Grey Cloak released him, and the dragon splashed down into the water.

Hacking, coughing, and fanning the smoke out of his face, Grey Cloak said, "That was a dirty trick, Streak!" He moved out of the smoke and hacked a few times. "That's it. Every man, elf, and dragon for himself!"

All chaos erupted in the fountain. Grey Cloak tripped Dyphestive, and a frog hopped over him. Grey Cloak spotted Streak poised to strike at the silver fish, dove at it, and scared it away.

As Streak agilely turned in the water to pursue it, Grey Cloak grabbed his tail again and slung the dragon out of the fountain. "No you don't, cheater!"

Streak landed on his side, rolled to a stop, and popped back up, poised to strike with his pink tongue flickering.

Grey Cloak pointed and laughed at his dragon. "Ah-hahaha, that's what you get, you little bug muncher."

"Gang way!" Dyphestive came out of nowhere and plowed right over Grey Cloak.

The fountain became a battlefield. Within moments, Grey Cloak, Dyphestive, and Streak had tripped, tugged, bumped, tackled, bit, punched, and dunked one another in pursuit of the silver fish.

All of them went at it with a feverish look in their eyes. Water and goldfish flew over the fountain's rim.

The longer they chased the silver fish, the more obsessed they became. The playful punching and tripping became more violent as they clawed their way on top of one another. They were like piranhas hunting for fresh meat.

Grey Cloak found a goldfish in his hand, tapped Dyphestive on the shoulder, and slapped him in the face the moment his brother turned. Dyphestive roared like a hungry bear.

Grey Cloak stuffed the fish in his brother's mouth. "Enjoy your filet." He wiggled by his brother and dove at the silver fish again.

Dyphestive pulled a fish out by the tail. It was a patchwork of black and gold. It wriggled in his mitt. He flung it at Grey Cloak's head. The effort was errant, as it sailed over Grey Cloak, who ducked, and hit Tatiana square in the face.

Tatiana's face reddened as she boiled over with anger and said in an all-powerful voice, "That's enough!" Her voice shook the very fountain's waters, causing it to sputter and spit for a moment.

Grey Cloak, Dyphestive, and Streak stopped in their tracks.

"What are you fools doing?" Tatiana demanded. "Get out of that fountain!" There were several fish flapping and jumping on the wet tile floor. "And put those back in. What is this, a halfling nursery?"

Grey Cloak rubbed his eyes and rolled his neck. His head was light and hazy. He wasn't sure what had come over him, and his jaw was sore. He stepped out of the fountain, dripping water all over the floor, and started helping his brother pick up the fish. He dropped them into the fountain one by one. "Where have you been?"

With a frown and crossed arms, she said, "About."

"Oh." He tossed another fish in the water. "Thanks for filling in all the details."

Tatiana approached the fountain and looked down into the clear water at the schools of goldfish. "You were playing with the silver fish, I see. Many have tried to catch it. All have failed, including me." She managed a wry smile. "It's a tricky fish."

Grey Cloak took off his shirt and wrung it out. "You can say that again." He slung his hair out of his eyes. "That fish made us crazy. I've got a sore jaw thanks to big elbows over there and that fish." He eyed Dyphestive, who was shaking himself like a dog. "What is that fish? It's not like the others."

"No one knows. Perhaps it's an aberration of the goldfish spawn." She dipped her fingers into the water. "Perhaps it appeared by magic. One thing is for certain. No one can catch it."

Grey Cloak grabbed a dagger from his belt on the floor. He charged it with wizardry fire and leaned over the pool. "I have an idea."

Tatiana pushed his hand aside. "Don't you dare. You'll kill the goldfish."

He put the dagger away and sighed. "Fine." He looked her up and down. Tatiana was very beautiful, and her snug wizard clothing only enhanced her handsome womanly figure. He wanted to shove her in the pool. "Is there a reason for your arrival?"

"Yes, you need to come with me." She looked him up and down. "But we need to dry you off first. You must be presentable. Get your dragon."

Streak lingered under the water at the fountain's edge. His eyes were locked on the silver fish.

When Grey Cloak reached into the water to grab him, Streak snapped at him. "Whoa! Streak, get out of there!"

The dragon swam away.

Tatiana shook her head. "Can't you control your dragon?"

Grey Cloak replied, "He'll be fine. Let him play." He gathered up his clothing and gear. "Lead the way, Tatiana. I can't wait to meet your mysterious family. Do they have many horns and extra teeth?"

"Ha ha," she said.

He caught Dyphestive staring into the fountain with a worried expression. "Come on, Dyphestive. He won't come out until he's ready. He's a stubborn dragon."

Dyphestive dropped his long arm down toward the water. "But..."

"But nothing. Come on before he bites your finger off," Grey Cloak added. "Besides, I think Tatiana is going to feed us something other than goldfish, right, Tatiana?"

"Oh, of course," she said.

Dyphestive finally pulled his gaze away and hurried along.

Led by Tatiana, the trio walked right into one of the murals, leaving Streak and the fountain alone.

11

The moment Grey Cloak passed under the archway, the mural changed from leagues of flowery fields at dusk to a dreary stairwell made of gray stone. The stone steps were made of black obsidian marble, and they flowed up along the inside of the tower's main wall. The trio was sealed in on both sides.

Tatiana continued to lead the way upward. Her footfalls were quiet, and she breathed easily. They walked nonstop for several long minutes, slowly winding upward toward the top of the tower.

"One would think that wizards would have a more efficient way to travel from one level to another," Grey Cloak quipped.

"Even mages are dedicated to some level of conditioning," Tatiana said as she looked at him over her shoulder. "Do you tire?"

"Not at all. I was more concerned about the length of the journey. I'm not very comfortable with being in close quarters with you for a long time," he said.

"It sounds as if you're growing fond me."

"I'd agree if your mere presence didn't make my skin want to crawl off my bones." Grey Cloak heard Dyphestive chuckle. "But if that's your measure of fondness, then yes, I'm very fond."

The truth was he was becoming fonder of her. Tatiana's beauty was hard to ignore, and it could easily overcome a younger man's impulses. The slight sway of her hips captured his attention on the way up. *She's a witch, remember. Don't let her bewitch you, Grey Cloak.*

To put his mind on something else, he ran his fingers across the stone walls. They were as cold as frost. He cast a nervous look at Dyphestive.

Dyphestive returned his stare with a perplexed look of his own. He touched the wall with his sausage-link fingers. "Chilly."

"Ahem," Grey Cloak said as he fell back a few steps from Tatiana. "But will it be much longer? I feel like I've been in the tower a lifetime, but I haven't aged a day."

"Consider it a blessing." She walked with her robes hiked up over her ankles. "The Wizard Watch does wonders for the aging process. It's a place where you can come, stay as long as you like, and relax."

"I thought this was where you came to train," Grey Cloak said.

"Absolutely. The Wizard Watch accommodates all of our daily needs."

Grey Cloak raised his eyebrows. He wasn't a dwarf, who were notorious for measuring time and distance blindfolded, but he had no doubts that they should've reached the very top of the tower long ago. The laborious walking wasn't as tiresome on his legs as it was on his mind. His back muscles tightened.

Something's wrong.

"Tatiana, seriously, if this is some sort of test or game, it needs to stop. We could have walked to the top of the tower three times over by now." He stopped suddenly. Dyphestive bumped into him. He ignored it and said, "Explain yourself."

Tatiana stopped and turned. "We're almost there." With a nod, she said, "Come and see for yourself."

Grey Cloak and Dyphestive eased their way up the steps. Around the bend, several yards up, was a black obsidian door with two smokeless bronze torches bracketed on each side. Underneath the torches were two figures covered in hooded crimson robes. Grey Cloak couldn't see their hands or faces, but they appeared to hover above the ground.

"Who are they?" Grey Cloak asked.

"Portal Guardians," she said. "We don't have anything to fear from them so long as we have permission to enter the chambers on the other side. Which, I assure you, we do." Her fingers dusted across Grey Cloak's elbow as she resumed her trek. "I hope you understand that it's not my desire to make you uncomfortable. I know the Wizard Watch is foreign to you and very strange to those who are not accustomed to it. Its inner workings are unique, but I assure you that it's for your safety."

"Thanks, Tatiana, that's very comforting," Grey Cloak said as they made it to the top landing. "I feel worse already."

She rolled her eyes and sighed. "Are we ever going to get along?"

"I doubt it, but don't you quit dreaming." He smirked.

Tatiana took center stage in front of the black obsidian door. With her fingertip, she traced arcane symbols on the door. Her fingers left a bright burning trail that slowly faded.

Grey Cloak studied her every move and locked it into his memory as he repeated the motions in his mind.

The black obsidian door faded, and a gust of chill wind blasted their faces.

With the wind rustling his hair, he shouted to Tatiana, "In there?"

She nodded. "I'll go first." She led the way.

The blood brothers followed. The black door re-formed behind them, and the wind stopped. They were outside on a huge stone platform just beneath the passing clouds. The air was as chill as winter.

Tatiana led them up a small flight of steps to the very top of the tower. The girth of the tower top was startling. It was at least one hundred yards long and just as wide. It dwarfed the Wizard Watch tower that they'd seen from the outside.

Grey Cloak's nape hairs stood on end as he locked his eyes on the huge black bulk of scales that almost covered the platform from end to end. It came to life and became the biggest dragon he'd ever seen.

The dragon reared up to its full height and glared down on them with flaming-blue eyes.

"It can't be," Dyphestive uttered as he tightened his grip on his war mace, Thunderash.

Grey Cloak had no doubt in his mind who the all-powerful behemoth was. They were face-to-face with Black Frost.

12

Dyphestive was out of the blocks and charging Black Frost like a bull. He had Thunderash cocked behind his shoulder, and as soon as he reached Black Frost's foot, he swung.

The head of the war mace hit the dragon's foot and made a loud *Craaaaack!*

Black Frost, towering several stories above all of them, stood unfazed as Dyphestive clobbered his toes and feet over and over again.

Tatiana stood beside Grey Cloak with the Star of Light burning in her grip.

Grey Cloak's own fingers were locked on the Figurine of Heroes as he stared down inevitable doom. He started to spit the words from his mouth, but in the middle of his summoning, he paused.

"What are you doing?" Tatiana asked with a bewildered look. "Are you going to summon help? Hurry!"

He loosened his grip on the figurine and left it inside the Cloak of Legends's pocket. He narrowed his eyes on his surroundings. Black Frost hadn't made a sound, not even the softest scuffle of talon scraping over stone. No heat or icy cold came from the dragon's body. Instead, Black Frost looked down on them, eyes burning but without recognition.

"Do something, Grey Cloak," Tatiana said. "Use the figurine."

"Funny that you would suggest that given your hatred of the figurine," he said.

"Our plight is desperate!" she said.

Grey Cloak closed his eyes. It was difficult to get a feel for the room, but he wasn't outside. He could tell that much. The chamber echoed with every strike of Dyphestive's mace. The walls reverberated from the sound. He opened his eyes. Black Frost was gone. They were inside with a fountain much like the one where they'd started. Instead of four walls with murals in the archways, this one had eight walls, shaping the room into an octagon. Curtains were drawn in front of each.

"Huh, a grand illusion. I should have caught that sooner," he said.

Dyphestive was still hammering away at the floor. He stopped, gawked, and blinked his eyes. "What happened?"

Grey Cloak whisked a dagger out of its sheath and pointed it at Tatiana. "We've been duped by our dear friend. That's what happened."

Dyphestive rubbed his eyes. "Why?"

"Because they want the Figurine of Heroes, but I don't think they know the words. They wanted me to say them. Isn't that right, Tatiana?"

She shrugged. "If I needed the words, I could retrieve them from Dalsay."

"Oh, put your dagger away, child. There's no need for more discourse. It was merely a test."

Grey Cloak turned and faced the source of the mysterious voice. An elf unlike any he'd seen before sat on the fountain's edge. He had the refined features of elvenkind, but one side of his silky locks was white, and the other side was black. His face was youthful and energetic, and his eyes were dark and spacey. His beard was cropped with silver bands around the black hair. He wore black-and-white-checkered robes and rested his slender fingers on a black wooden cane with a polished silver handle.

"Let me guess. You're Tatiana's father," Grey Cloak said.

"No," the elf said politely. He pushed off of his cane to stand. "I'm Gossamer, the high mage of this Wizard Watch tower." He walked over with his cane clicking on the floor and extended his hand. "A pleasure to meet you."

Grey Cloak shook Gossamer's ice-cold hand. "You're as icy as Tatiana."

"I hope not." Gossamer gave Dyphestive's hand a firm shake. "You *are* a big one."

"Thank you," Dyphestive said with his chin up.

"Eh, first things first. The Figurine of Heroes," Gossamer began. "I noticed that the first item you reached for was the Figurine of Heroes when you were confronted by Black Frost."

"So? It was Black Frost. What else would I do?" Grey Cloak asked.

"Is he that big?" Dyphestive asked.

"According to our sources, Black Frost is every bit as big as that and getting bigger. That bauble"—he eyed Grey Cloak—"will hardly be enough to stop him."

"Then why do you want it?" Grey Cloak asked.

"The Figurine of Heroes is an artifact of unsearchable power. It is property of the Wizard Watch." Gossamer was a smooth talker, but he had a bite to his tone. "If we can understand how it opens and closes portals to other worlds, it might help us put a stop to Black Frost."

Grey Cloak raised a brow. "Are you telling me that you didn't create the figurine?"

"No, we did create it, but magic contains many unpredictable powers. We've yet to master them. Dalsay was allowed to use it to test its properties." Tatiana shot Gossamer a surprised look. "We never foresaw that the consequences could be fatal to our own."

"What else would you expect when you open a portal to another dimension?" Dyphestive asked.

Everyone looked at the hulking youth.

Dyphestive shrugged. "What? I pay attention." He scratched his chin with his index finger. "Why don't you make another one?"

"As much as I hate to confess it, its creation is just as much of an accident as it is of design," Gossamer admitted. "A council of the most prominent members of the Wizard Watch worked in tandem to create it." His expression turned grave. "Several died in the process, and others vanished."

"And you let Dalsay run around with that thing?" Tatiana asked. "It killed all my brothers, who were fetching your precious dragon charms, and to what end? Death!"

Grey Cloak found some relief in the fact that Tatiana didn't know any more about the figurine than he did. *Maybe the batty ole elf isn't so bad.* "It's saved more lives than it's taken since I've had it."

"That was our hope when we sent it out with Dalsay," Gossamer said regretfully. "No one is more sorrowful for your loss than I, Tatiana." He touched her shoulder. "I hope you believe that."

She moved away.

13

Gossamer slowly strolled around the room with Grey Cloak and Dyphestive in tow. He eyed Dyphestive. "You are very insightful for such a brute. What else is rattling around in that thick skull of yours?"

"Well, I was thinking that creating the figurine might have had something to do with opening the portal that Black Frost gains his power from," Dyphestive said.

"Ah," Gossamer commented. "And?"

"Maybe you've come to the conclusion that destroying the figurine might destroy Black Frost," Dyphestive finished.

"Impressive." Gossamer nudged Grey Cloak. "I see you aren't the only bright mind in the tandem. However, the energy source that Black Frost taps into has no direct connection to the figurine."

Good, Grey Cloak thought. He didn't want to have a good reason to give up the figurine. He'd become used to having it. "Where is the source of his power? Why don't you destroy that?"

"We believe the very source of Black Frost's power comes from Dark Mountain." Gossamer approached one of the arches. Forest-green curtains hung inside the archway. With a subtle wave of his hand, the curtains parted.

"Whoa," Dyphestive said.

They were staring at a lifelike mural that showed an aerial view of Dark Mountain's stark terrain. The jagged spires of the black mountain range were peppered with volcanoes spitting out streams of bright-orange molten lava. Gray clouds hung in the sky, blocking the sun, and the highest peaks were covered in frost and banks of snow.

A chill raced down Grey Cloak's spine. If there were ever a place that he hated, it would be Dark Mountain. Raised there most of his life, he only remembered it as a place of misery.

The mural shifted, and the image zoomed in closer to Dark Mountain, as if they were gliding through the sky.

Gossamer pointed at the ziggurat in the top levels of the mountains. The gargantuan stone structure overlooked Dark Mountain's valley. Chiseled right out of the mountain stone, the ominous temple dwarfed any building in Gapoli. As the mural panned in closer, a full view of the temple's top was cast in full light. Dragons were perched on the ledge of Black Frost's temple like battlements. Facing outward, they were the guardians protecting Black Frost and the temple. Dozens stood perfectly spaced along the temple's rim. Both middling and grand dragons were posted on the corners. They were nothing compared to Black Frost.

"Sweet potatoes, look at the size of him," Dyphestive said with awe.

It seemed like an odd statement, considering they'd just seen an illusion of Black Frost earlier, but even Grey Cloak had to agree. Compared to the other dragons, Black Frost was tremendous. It seemed as though an entire thunder of dragons could ride on his back.

Grey Cloak stretched his hand toward the mural that dwarfed him in size. "Is this real?"

Gossamer leaned on his cane. "No, this is a simulation of what we know." He pointed at the mural with his cane. "Long ago, the temple that supports Black Frost's girth was accessible to all. The citizens of Dark Mountain used it as a place to worship the dragons. Decades ago, it was sealed off, when Black Frost gained power after the Day of Betrayal. We believe the power that Black Frost draws upon is inside the temple. People have differing theories, but the most accepted theory is that he and the rebellious wizards opened a portal using the murals, and he was able to tap into another world and drain it."

Grey Cloak and Dyphestive exchanged concerned

looks.

"What?" Gossamer asked.

"He's draining Thanadiliditis's world," Grey Cloak said. "Shouldn't you be talking to him?"

"We've tried, but he proves very elusive. We aren't so sure that he can do anything to help anyway. Black Frost is becoming omnipotent. If he continues to feed, how long will it be before he feeds on this world?"

"Won't he become full?" Dyphestive asked.

"One would think so, but that's the problem. Black Frost does not fill. He keeps growing." Gossamer tapped his cane on the image of the temple. "The truth is that we weren't so worried about him at first. So long as he remained in Dark Mountain, he wasn't much of a problem. We relied on the Sky Riders to keep him in check. But lo and behold, he left his roost and all but annihilated them. His breath alone proved to be too much for the valiant fighters of the sky. He even killed the Gunder giants."

Grey Cloak thought about Tontor, the shaggy-haired giant he'd met on the island. "All of them?" he asked.

Gossamer shrugged, staring at the temple. "We planted spies in Dark Mountain to seek out the secrets of the temple. It's been years since we've heard back from any of them."

"They're dead?" Dyphestive asked.

"Possibly, or they joined Black Frost. His popularity has grown quite fashionable of late."

Tatiana stormed over. "Are you telling me that members of the Wizard Watch have joined forces with Black Frost?"

Gossamer arched a brow. "Don't be naive, Tatiana. You know that the Wizard Watch's role remains neutral in Gapoli. We strive to maintain a balance for the greater good, but not all of us see it that way."

Tatiana's fists balled at her sides. "And I take it that killing Black Frost is for the greater good?"

"Of course," Gossamer said politely. "He is a threat to everything that exists. But no doubt, members of the watch have been aiding him. It would be a slip in judgment to assume otherwise."

"Unless you already made the assumption and paid for it," Grey Cloak said.

"Even wizards make mistakes," Gossamer said. He cleared his throat. "I don't deny the error of our ways. We are trying to fix them."

"Some of us are. Some aren't, it sounds like," Tatiana said. "There's no telling who's on whose side, as so many of us come and go from tower to tower."

"So many of who?" Grey Cloak asked. "This tower is huge, and we're the only people I've seen. Where is everyone else?"

"About," Gossamer offered. "Now, if you will, we need some trustworthy allies to enter Black Frost's temple and figure out his secret." He eyed Grey Cloak and Dyphestive. "We want you to do it."

14

"Are you out of your skull?" Grey Cloak raised his voice so loud that it surprised him. "We aren't going back to Dark Mountain. Not now, not ever!"

Gossamer's eyes widened. "Hear me out."

Grey Cloak shook his head and poked a finger at the elven wizard. "No, you hear me out. I didn't come here to do the will of the Wizard Watch. All you've done, in my experience, is send us on a bunch of fruitless adventures. Speaking of which, where are the dragon charms that we recovered? Huh? The only reason I came here was to figure out what happened to them. Well, Gossamer, where are they?"

Gossamer searched everyone's intense stares. "If you agree to go to Dark Mountain, I'll tell you."

Grey Cloak's cheeks flushed, but before he exploded,

Dyphestive stepped in front of him. "Tell us about the dragon charms first."

"And if I do, you'll go to Dark Mountain?" Gossamer asked.

Grey Cloak moved in front of Dyphestive. "We'll consider it. But first I want to know how you propose to get us back and forth from there. It will take weeks to travel, not to mention, Monarch City's northern bridge has fallen."

Gossamer clicked his cane on the floor. "We have our ways around that." With a wave of his hand, the other seven curtains opened. Six of them revealed identical views to the fountain chamber they were standing in. It was like looking into a mirror, but their own reflections weren't there. "The Wizard Watch possesses a unique opportunity for travel. We have a tower in every territory, and these separate archways will take you to them."

Grey Cloak rubbed his chin. "Ah, that will save a lot of travel time. But that's not going to get us inside the most heavily guarded temple fortress in the world."

"No, it won't, but we'll aid you the best we can." Gossamer eyeballed Grey Cloak's cloak. "I can see that you're very well equipped as is."

"You do know that everyone in Dark Mountain is looking for us, don't you?" Grey Cloak asked sarcastically. "We've been there most of our lives, and it isn't very easy to blend in, not to mention get close to the temple."

"We've considered all things," Gossamer replied. "You'll

be well equipped. We need someone who we can trust, and Tatiana has vouched for both of you."

Grey Cloak slid his gaze her way, but she didn't look at him. *She's full of surprises, isn't she?* "I'm confident that I can go it alone, but I can't do it with this moose tagging along. No offense, Dy, but well, you know, you're big."

"Where you go, I go," Dyphestive insisted in his deep voice.

"Naturally," Grey Cloak said as he spied another mural with the curtains still closed. He walked over to the archway and parted the curtains. As he pulled one side back, the other side parted easily. The huge mural quickly flashed numerous images of different places at all times of the day, all over the world. He stretched his fingers toward it.

"Don't touch that portal," Gossamer warned.

Grey Cloak held his hand out just short of the mural. The entire world was passing by in split seconds.

Gossamer stood beside him. "We opened this portal with the hope that we could travel back in time and stop Black Frost before he acquired his power."

"What happened?" Dyphestive asked.

"I'll tell you what happened. Much like the maligned Figurine of Heroes, we have no control over what happens." Gossamer tapped his cane twice. "What you are seeing is the past, present, and future. You could wind up a thousand years forward or a thousand years back. Everyone who has entered has been lost to us."

"How many have entered?" Grey Cloak asked.

"Three that I know of." Gossamer frowned. "None have been seen or heard from again. We don't know if they survived or not."

"Can you close it?" Dyphestive asked.

"No, the Wizard Watch keeps it open for further study. I can't say I blame them. Times are desperate. We hoped the figurine would provide us with a force that could match Black Frost and his Riskers, but as we all well know, it's unpredictable." Gossamer sighed. "All we can do now is keep looking for answers," he said.

"What about the dragon charms?" Grey Cloak asked. "I'd like an answer to that."

15

Gossamer moved away from the scenes flashing inside the mural. With a wave of his cane, the curtain glided shut, and he approached the fountain. "We have many dragon charms," he admitted as he stared into the waters shining in the fountain's pool. He sat down on the fountain's rim. "The problem is that we don't have as many as Black Frost."

Grey Cloak approached. "Might I ask where the dragon charms are?"

With a wave of his cane, the waters at the top of the fountain began to increase in pressure and burble. In between the three ornamental fish spitting water, a strange object rose.

Grey Cloak and the others tilted their heads to one side.

A warrior's open-faced helmet rose from the spring. It

was bright with energy that glowed from the gemstones attached to it. The precious stones shone like rubies, emeralds, pearls, and sapphires. There was no mistaking their uniqueness and flat, oval shapes. They were dragon stones.

"It's beautiful," Dyphestive said, his eyes fastened on the helmet. "It makes Codd's helmet look like goblin craft."

Even Grey Cloak marveled at the object's beauty. He counted ten dragon charms in all fastened to the helmet, which slowly spun in the air. Six stones made a ring around the helmet's rim. Two more were fastened on the cheek plates, and the last two on the back plate that covered the neck. "That's a very surprising configuration, Gossamer. Not to mention, that isn't very many stones. I've seen dozens on the chest of Black Frost's Riskers. Is that all we have?"

Gossamer swiped at the long strands of hair that fell over his eye. "There are a few more, but the rest of the suit is still being assembled."

"Suit?" Dyphestive asked.

"We realize we don't have the same number of charms that Black Frost does. His dragon riders are composed of *naturals* like the two of you, who lead the other Riskers that rely on the use of the dragon charms."

"So, the more dragon charms he has, the more dragons he controls?" Dyphestive asked.

"An obvious truth, but we believe there's more to it than that." Gossamer stood and eyed the glimmering helmet.

"We believe that Black Frost desires the charms because of their ability to control dragons."

Tatiana's face brightened. "He fears that the dragon charms could control him."

Gossamer gave an approving nod. "We theorize that if we can use a large set of dragon stones in tandem, we could control Black Frost."

Grey Cloak stood on the fountain's edge, looking at the helmet, and said, "Have you tried?"

"No. The problem is that we don't have any dragons, and we also feel that this ability would be best suited for a natural. It was our hope to reveal this to the Sky Riders, but that plan failed when Black Frost eliminated them."

"What about Anya? She's a Sky Rider," Dyphestive suggested.

"Oh, I don't think so. She'd rather die than trust the likes of us," Tatiana insisted.

Grey Cloak had the answers he'd been looking for. Gossamer had given him a reasonable explanation about the dragon charms, and as crazy as combining all of their properties at once sounded, it might just work. He made a quick suggestion, "Do you want me to try it?"

16

Everyone looked at him, and Gossamer said, "As I stated, we don't have any dragons to try it on, aside from your dragon, Streak, but you already control him."

"True, and he has the ability to control other dragons," Grey Cloak offered. "Perhaps the both of us could do it."

Gossamer closed his eyes and tapped his cane quietly on the floor. He took a deep breath in and let it out. "Your runt is a crypt dragon, is he not?"

"He's a controller, yes. He took over a grand with little effort."

Gossamer opened his eyes. "I have no way of knowing how this will work without it being tested." He shook his head. "It's too dangerous, and if Black Frost learns of this deceit, he'll be able to turn it against us. Our situation is already dire enough."

"Even if you have more dragon charms, you won't know if the helmet will work or not. Let me test it," Grey Cloak pleaded. "I can at least get close enough to test it out on him. I'll do it."

"And I'll help him," Dyphestive offered.

Gossamer stood. "I'll discuss this with the Wizard Watch. In the meantime, rest." He eyed Tatiana. "Keep them entertained." He walked through one of the archways into an identical room and vanished.

Dyphestive's gaze followed after the black-and-white elf. "Where did that take him?"

"To the Wizard Watch near Loose Boot. Many mages are gathered there in council," she said. "Is anyone hungry?"

"No," Grey Cloak said.

"I am," Dyphestive added.

"I'll have food brought." She looked at Grey Cloak. "You don't eat much, do you?"

"No. Could I fetch Streak? Wherever I'm going, he's coming."

She eyed the fountain. "He should be right where you left him."

"That's not the same fountain, is it?" Dyphestive looked into the water. "The other fountain had two fish, and this one has three fish at the top."

Streak slunk out of the water to the fountain's rim. He spit a stream of water at Dyphestive.

"Will you stop that?" Dyphestive said. "Grey, get your dragon. He's being ornery."

Streak splashed Dyphestive with his tail.

"See?" the brawny blood brother said.

Grey Cloak strolled over and peered into the fountain. It was the same size as the other one and filled with gold-fish. He could have sworn it was on the floor below them, however. He glanced at Tatiana. "I'm not even going to ask."

"It's probably for the better," she said.

He hauled the dripping dragon out of the water.

Streak shivered and shed the water. His tongue flicked out of his mouth and licked Grey Cloak's face.

"Someone's acting awfully spry," Grey Cloak said. He lifted the dragon up a little higher. "And feeling heavier too. How many fish did you eat?"

Streak offered an answer with a deadpan stare.

"I see." He let Streak crawl underneath his cloak and latch onto his back. He winced. "Ow."

Tatiana grimaced. "Does he dig those claws into you every time?"

"My shirt is thick, but yes," he answered. "Tatiana, if I didn't know any better, I'd say that you're in the dark about things as much as we are."

"There is much truth to that." Her eye twitched. "I'm really disappointed about the figurine. It has caused more harm than good. They never should've let it out of the towers. We were only an experiment. My brothers were an experiment."

"Do you really trust these people?" Grey Cloak asked.

"I trust Dalsay, and I trust Gossamer." She cast a look at the brothers. "And even though it's hard to say it, I trust both of you. It's probably an error in judgment in your case." She eyed Grey Cloak. "But I have to learn to take risks."

"That's very touching," Grey Cloak said dryly.

Dyphestive gave her a crushing hug that lifted her off her toes. "I trust you too."

Gasping, she patted Dyphestive on the back. "You're crushing me."

Dyphestive let her go. "Sorry. I couldn't have done that if Leena was about." He glanced over his shoulder. "I've wanted to do that for a while."

Tatiana blushed.

Dyphestive waved his hands and fumbled for words. "Not like that. I mean, you're astonishing. It's just, well, you're my friend. I wanted to show you in case I don't get another chance."

She kissed his cheek. "I'm flattered."

A male elf dressed in deep-purple servant's clothing underneath a white apron pushed a cart of food through one of the tower's archways. He pushed the cart halfway into the room and departed in the direction he came.

The cart was covered in silver serving platters and glass carafes full of wine and juice.

Dyphestive lifted the lid off one of the platters. Steam rose from underneath the silvery dome, and he licked his lips. "Cooked venison." He peeled a hunk off and started to eat. "Mmmm. I love venison."

Streak popped his head out from Grey Cloak's cloak and sniffed, his tongue flickering out of his mouth. He slithered down Grey Cloak's back, headed to Dyphestive, and rose up on his hind legs, his tail sweeping the floor behind him.

Dyphestive dropped hunks of meat into the hungry dragon's mouth. Streak's jaws clacked shut with every bite. "It's like feeding those moat monsters back at Monarch Castle," Dyphestive said with a playful grin.

Tatiana poured herself a glass of wine and offered Grey Cloak a sample. "Yes? No?"

"I'll pass." He sat down on the fountain's edge and eyeballed the goldfish. He saw no sign of the silver fish. "This isn't the same fountain."

Tatiana joined him. "They're all the same."

"This is a strange place." Grey Cloak eyed the ominous midnight ceiling that glowed with colorful stars. "I don't think I would like to live here." His nostrils flared. "It smells funny."

She sniffed. "I don't smell anything."

"That's what I mean. It should smell like something aside from a room with eight walls."

Gossamer ran back into the room from a different archway than the one he'd left through. His face was flushed, and his chest heaved. "Time to run. They come!"

17

"What are you talking about, Gossamer?" Tatiana asked. "Who comes?"

Gossamer hurried over to the fountain with his cane clicking on the floor. He stretched out his hand toward the dragon-charm helm. "We deliberated for hours, but their hearts are as hard as stone."

"Did you say hours?" Grey Cloak asked. "You haven't been gone that long." He looked at Dyphestive. "Has he?"

Dyphestive shrugged as he swallowed another hunk of venison and wiped his mouth with a white tablecloth. "It didn't seem so."

The dragon-charm helm floated into Gossamer's waiting arms. He cradled it to his chest. "Needless to say, they did not like the idea of sending Grey Cloak and Dyphestive to Dark Mountain with the helm." He eyed Grey Cloak. "But they also demanded the Figurine of Heroes."

Grey Cloak gathered up Streak, letting the dragon latch onto his back. "We're out of here. Dyphestive, let's go." He scanned the room. "Tat, how do we get out of here?"

Gossamer shared a grim expression. "That won't be possible. All of the passages are sealed by wizard magic." He tossed the helmet to Grey Cloak. His eyes slid over to the huge mural of flashing images. "There's only one way out, through the mural of time."

Grey Cloak looked at the time mural. "We're not going through there. We'll take our chances elsewhere. Let's go, Dyphestive."

The blood brothers dashed into one of the identical alcoves and found themselves in the same fountain chamber they'd been in with Tatiana and Gossamer.

Gossamer pleaded with him, "I tell you there is no way out except the time mural. You must go."

Grey Cloak and Dyphestive dashed through one strange archway after another only to find themselves in the same room where they'd started. "This is madness." He pointed a finger at Tatiana. "You know how to get us out of here. Get us out!"

Tatiana blanched. "I'm sorry, but I cannot. The Wizard Watch has acted, and only they can let you out."

Grey Cloak faced the time mural. It presented an

opportunity to start all over, in the past or the future. *I can't leave my friends behind. That would be wrong.* He handed the helmet to Dyphestive. "Hold on to this." He stood in front of the time mural and faced Gossamer. "We'll wait for the rest of your brood and see what they have to say."

Gossamer shook his head. "A bad spirit stands among them. You should leave now, while you have a chance. Take a leap of faith. I have."

Dyphestive whispered to his brother, "Should we do it? I'll do it if you do."

"We can't leave the others."

"I don't think we have a choice. They'd understand. Tatiana will explain it to them." Dyphestive eyed her. "Won't you?"

"Of course," Tatiana replied.

A host of mages entered the chamber from one of the other archways. All of them wore robes like drapery in an assortment of colors. The tallest of them wore black robes with silver trim and a tall pointed hood over her head. She was human, with piercing-blue eyes, a frosty expression, and flowing silver-blond hair. The others stood behind her.

"I am Uruiah," the tall blond mage said, "highest of the Wizard Watch. You are Grey Cloak, son of Zanna Paydark." She glanced at Dyphestive. "And you are the son of Olgstern Stronghair." She eyed the helmet. "You have something that belongs to us."

Dyphestive held the helmet toward the time mural. "Let us be, or I'll drop it in."

Uruiah tossed her head back and laughed. "Do as you will. We have no use for that." She turned her attention to Grey Cloak. "It's the Figurine of Heroes that we want. It was our desire that you would give it up freely, but you've proved too greedy to part with it. Return it to us of your own free will, and you will be allowed to depart unscathed."

Grey Cloak rubbed his chin. "And we can keep the helmet?"

"No," she said.

"But you said that you had no use for it," he fired back.

Uruiah's eyes narrowed. "Don't toy with me. Hand over the figurine."

"Don't do it!" Gossamer said. "They're in league with Black Frost."

"What?" Tatiana asked. "That can't be."

"Yes, they are. They're traitors to the Wizard Watch. Uruiah is the largest disappointment of all." Gossamer glared at her. "She sold out, the same as the Sky Riders did on the Day of Betrayal. I didn't want to believe it until I heard it from her own lips."

Uruiah smiled. "I made you an offer, Gossamer. You shouldn't have refused. Your refusal shall prove fatal."

A score of soldiers wearing crimson tunics over chainmail stormed into the room from the other archways. They wore the open-faced, hard angular helmets of the Dark Mountain's Black Guard. They hemmed Gossamer and Tatiana in by the fountain.

Uruiah pointed to Gossamer and Tatiana and said to the Black Guard, "Kill them."

18

"No, wait!" Grey Cloak said. He reached inside his pocket for the figurine. "Let them be, and I'll give it to you. Then you let us be."

Uruiah sawed her slender finger over her cheek. "I'm a reasonable person. If they swear allegiance to the forces of Dark Mountain, they'll be spared."

"That's not part of the deal," Grey Cloak said. *Buy time. Buy time. Buy time.* At that point, he had no doubt that Uruiah would kill all of them or turn them in to Black Frost. *I have to figure out another way.* "Listen, be reasonable. Without these objects, we aren't a threat to you or Black Frost. You get the figurine and the dragon-charm helm. Let us go. We'll part ways, and you'll never see us again."

"Take the portal!" Gossamer said. "Don't be a fool. You're making a deal with a demon." A Black Guard knocked Gossamer in the back of the head with the pommel of his sword. Gossamer sank to the ground.

Tatiana rushed toward Gossamer, but two Black Guards seized her by the arms and yanked her away. "Unhand me before I turn you to ashes."

"How delightful. I like you, Tatiana. You always were a fighter." Uruiah's hand glowed. A ball of energy formed in her palm that shone like a ruby rosebud. She tossed it at Tatiana's belly.

The sorceress let out a shriek, and her eyes rolled up in her head. She spasmed violently, and her head dropped down to her chest.

"You witch!" Dyphestive moved forward. "I should pummel you!"

"Ah, but you wouldn't do that, would you, sweet Dyphestive?" Uruiah asked.

"Don't be so sure. I killed Draykis."

Uruiah's eyes widened. "There is no way out. Be wise and surrender."

"Never! You surrender!" Dyphestive argued back.

While the others were engaged, Grey Cloak calculated his chances. *Option one, take the portal to freedom, but Tatiana and Gossamer will still be killed. Option two, fight superior numbers, but at least one of us will die. Option three, use the figurine, and even the odds.* He reached inside his cloak pocket and latched onto the figurine. *I knew it would be option three.* Concealing himself behind Dyphestive, he started uttering the arcane words of summoning.

Tatiana lifted her sagging chin and caught his eye. Her pleading eyes said, *Noooooo.*

Grey Cloak turned an angry stare at Uruiah. "You never should have hurt her." He dropped the Figurine of Heroes on the floor and watched Uruiah's eyes widen. "Say hello to my friend."

Uruiah's jaw tightened, and she and the wizard brood backed away from the smoking figurine. "Fool, we're prepared for your futile attempt." From underneath their floppy sleeves, well-crafted wands slid into their palms. She pointed her crooked wand at him. "I'll see to it that you're finished in the process."

The figurine stood upright as hazy black-and-gray smoke spit out of the top.

Streak popped his head out beside Grey Cloak's cloak for a moment then hid again.

With his fingertips tingling, Grey Cloak watched shadows emerge from the vapors. The smoke cleared, and everyone's gaze fell upon the two strange figures who stood among them.

They were men, of sorts, wearing pitch-black robes with traces of silver patterns delicately sewn into the fabric. Like birds, their heads tilted side to side as they studied their new surroundings. They had shocks of black hair, and their skin was gray and furry like a rat's. They stood nearly as big as men but were smallish in build. Their hands had black fingernails filed to points.

Dyphestive's Adam's apple rolled.

Grey Cloak's skin crawled. He sensed something strange about the smallish men. They were nothing like the others. Their sharp eyebrows and intense stares showed a countenance of evil. His heart skipped the moment they set their eyes upon him. One had silver eyes, and the other gold.

"Verbard," the one with golden eyes hissed. He spoke with cunning and intelligence.

"Yes, brother Catten?" the silver-eyed one with a wider face replied. When he spoke, he revealed sharp little teeth.

"We're back," Catten replied. He set his eyes on Grey Cloak. "What marvelous ears. I take it you summoned us to do your bidding."

He nodded.

Catten's and Verbard's eyes swept through the silent room. Their noses crinkled, and Verbard said, "This chamber reeks of good and evil." He eyed Uruiah. "These wizardlings carry wands. How pathetic."

"I sense our time is short, brother. Whatever shall we do?" Catten asked.

"Make the most of it." Verbard floated off the ground and faced Dyphestive. "I really don't like the looks of this one. I can only hope that we were summoned to kill him."

"Yes," Uruiah said. "Yes, you are. I am Uruiah, leader of

the Wizard Watch. You were summoned to serve the will of Black Frost and his wicked causes."

Catten rose a foot from the ground, floating above the floor. "The wizard with the little wand speaks." He nodded. "We are underlings. How is it that we were summoned?"

Uruiah's eyes fell on the Figurine of Heroes.

"I see." Catten needled his chin with his sharp fingernails. "Well, Uruiah, I would like to take a moment to inform you that we are Underling Lords Catten and Verbard." He showed his teeth. "And we don't serve anyone but ourselves."

Before Uruiah could blink, tendrils of lightning blasted from Catten's fingers and into Uruiah's chest. Her skin glowed so bright, the bones could be seen within. A chain of lightning spread from one mage to another. Wands went flying out of their hands.

For a brief moment, Grey Cloak thought they had an ally until Verbard turned on Dyphestive and said, "Let's kill them. Let's kill them all."

Lightning shot out of Verbard's fingertips and blasted straight through Dyphestive's chest. The fiery bolt lifted Dyphestive from the ground, and he flung his arms out. His jaw opened wide.

Without thinking, Grey Cloak charged the smallish man and jumped on him. He got the jolt of his life from his head to his toenails. He landed flat on his back in full spasms with fire running through his veins. *Zooks! These fiends are nasty.*

He rolled over on his side with his extremities cycling through numbness and pain. It hurt to even keep his eyes open. What he saw horrified him. Verbard and Catten were destroying every person in their path, and they set their eyes on Tatiana.

19

Dyphestive smelled the stink of his singed chest hairs as he fought his way back to his knees. His chest burned like a brush fire, and he tasted the tang of metal in his mouth. In the back of his mind, he knew that he should be dead. He wasn't. He lived.

With his jaw clenched, he stood with tremendous effort. Every move he made hurt, but it meant he was alive, alive and angry. He set his brooding stare on the visitors.

The moment he'd seen them, he'd known they were bad. He'd never seen such wickedness or natural evil on another creature's face. He snarled. Evil. He hated evil.

The chamber became a battleground with blood in the fountain's waters. The Black Guard and mages who had survived the initial onslaught fought for their lives. Many of them were blown out of their armor by javelins of lightning. Charred flesh smoldered on the tiled floor.

The underling named Catten faced off against two wand-wielding mages. Firepower blasted against firepower. The underling's expression was deadly and gleeful. His lightning shattered their wands and sent the mages flying backward into the walls.

Dyphestive spied his war mace lying on the floor nearby. With his ears ringing, he wandered over and picked it up in his big mitt. He set his gaze on Verbard, who'd turned his attention to Tatiana. "It's thunder time," he muttered. He lifted Thunderash up and charged.

Verbard turned in time to catch the blow of the war mace in his chest. The floating underling soared toward the curtain wall. He stopped before he hit it and sneered nastily. His eyes burned like molten silver as he looked at Dyphestive. "You're dead."

"I'm dead? He should be dead. I hit him with everything I had." Dyphestive stepped in front of Tatiana. "Stay behind me. He's taken his best shot, and I've taken mine."

Tatiana pulled out the Star of Light and formed a shield of white light before them.

Strands of lightning blasted into the shield as Verbard floated back toward them. The blasts skipped, ricocheted, then crackled and sizzled. They made angry hissing noises as they drilled into the dome of light.

Dyphestive squinted as he watched the mystic shield's fabric chip and give way. "Keep it up, Tat!" he hollered.

Her voice cracked as she said, "I'm trying. He's all-powerful. Mercy!"

From out of nowhere, Uruiah rose up behind Verbard. She unleashed the full force of her wand into Verbard's back. The underling's arms flung wide, and he dropped to the ground.

Dyphestive lost sight of Verbard as several Black Guards charged him. Three of them came with drawn swords. He leaned into them and swung. The war mace collided with their fine steel in a loud ring of metal. One blade broke, and the others flew out of the warriors' grasps.

Dyphestive paid the price as a sword lanced the back of his shoulder and pierced him deeply. "Guh!"

Tatiana called out, "Dyphestive!" White fire burned in her eyes. Using the Star of Light, she sent his attacker backward with a jagged bolt of power that exploded from her fist.

Using his one good arm, Dyphestive clubbed his other two attackers with skull-cracking force. Both soldiers fell to the ground dead.

"Your shoulder. It's bad," she said.

"Not bad enough." He spun his club and searched out his enemy, Verbard.

The underling had risen from the floor and had Uruiah pinned down with strands of lightning. Uruiah's hands were flung wide, forming a shield that reflected the underling's energy. She let out a frightful, angry scream as his bolts of power lanced into her entirety. Her body couldn't handle his might. Her skin sank and shriveled. Her body exploded in a plume of ash.

Tatiana gasped. "She was one of the strongest of our kind."

Verbard spun in midair and faced them. "Then the end of your kind is near."

LORDS OF THE AIR! *Who are these underlings? What are these underlings?*

Before Grey Cloak could reach Tatiana, the golden-eyed underling, Catten, fixed his attention on Grey Cloak. Bolts of lightning blasted out of the underling's hands, sending Grey Cloak careening away. Grey Cloak sprang to the side and started running.

Floating in the air, Catten hurled silver javelins at him like it was some sort of game. The lightning blew hunks of floor right out from underneath Grey Cloak's feet. He dove for the cover of the fountain and watched the fish at the top be blown apart.

Catten cackled with evil glee.

Right before Grey Cloak's eyes, he watched the Wizard Watch and Black Guard be devastated. The underlings showed no mercy on their souls as they were blown to bits and pieces. He hid behind the fountain wall.

This has to end. It has to end. The figurine should have summoned them back by now.

But the figurine hadn't summoned the underlings back to the dimension from where they came. They were still present and destroying everything.

Grey Cloak peeked over the rim.

Catten floated toward him. "I see you, rodent. Come on out and die."

A pair of mages rose from among the fallen. They pointed their wands at Catten and said in tandem, "*Sinew eruptus.*"

Catten's body went rigid. His feet landed on the ground as stiff as a board.

The pair of mages, a man and woman in lavender robes trimmed in white, approached. Their brown hair was slicked back, revealing their handsome and scholarly features. They crept toward Catten one more step, and an invisible force ripped their wands from their grips.

Catten caught the wands in his hands.

The mages' shocked faces lasted long enough for Catten to point their wands back at them and say, "*Sinew eruptus.*" The mages exploded.

Grey Cloak sank down farther, his stomach turning into knots. *I'll never use the figurine again.*

20

"Tsk... tsk... tsk," Verbard said to his brother, Catten. "I was really hoping there would be more people to kill, but it appears there are only a few of them left."

Catten floated along by his brother's side. He scanned the archways. "Certainly there are more about. I presume they're cowering. In the meantime, we still have them." He set his golden gaze on the heroes.

Grey Cloak, Dyphestive, and Tatiana clustered together by the fountain, panting. Dyphestive stood tall and made a wall between the underlings and the fountain. "Take your best shot, underling."

Catten and Verbard glanced at one another and barked laughter. "The humans of this world are as arrogant as the humans of our world."

"True, brother. Shall we make another example out of

these?" Verbard asked as threads of lightning danced on his glowing fingertips.

Grey Cloak gathered himself on one knee and said underneath his breath, "Buy time. They can't last forever. The figurine will take them back."

"Do you hear that, Verbard? They're conspiring. I don't care for conspirators," Catten said. "Do you?"

Shoulder to shoulder, the brothers floated around the fountain with their long robes dragging over the ground. They faced off with the heroes twenty feet away. Eyeing the bulging muscles in Dyphestive's meaty arms, Verbard said, "I really hate the big one. I think I'll take him apart piece by piece."

"I'll gladly finish off the others," Catten remarked. The dragon-charm helm lying on the tiled floor nearby caught his eye. "What is this?" With a wave of his hand, the helm lifted off the ground and into his hands. His clawlike fingers cradled the brilliant object like it was a child. "How remarkable. It's gaudy but carries within it great power. How significant." He closed his eyes. In a hushed voice, he said, "Ah, yessss."

Streak squirted out from underneath Grey Cloak's clothing and slunk across the floor toward the underlings with his head lowered.

"Marvelous, I've summoned a little dragon," Catten said as his eyelids opened. "Come, little creature, and serve your new master."

"No!" Grey Cloak jumped on top of his dragon as Dyphestive leaped in front of him. Streak's claws scraped over the floor as he strained to make headway toward Catten.

With an upward wave of his hands, Verbard levitated Grey Cloak and Dyphestive from the floor.

Once again, Streak squirted out of Grey Cloak's arms and dropped to the floor. He crawled underneath Catten's feet and sat down.

"Get away from them, Streak! Run!" Grey Cloak said.

Streak sat like a gargoyle.

Verbard twirled one finger, and Grey Cloak and Dyphestive began to spin like tops. "Time to dance."

The blood brothers' airborne bodies slammed into one another.

Running into Dyphestive was like hitting a stone wall. "Watch it," Grey Cloak said.

"I can't help it," Dyphestive offered helplessly. Suddenly his eyes rolled up into his head until the whites of his eyes shone. He lifted his war mace up like a bat.

Verbard grinned evilly. "First, I'm going to let the big one bash the little one into porridge. Then I'll do worse to the big one."

Grey Cloak stopped in midair.

Dyphestive spun like a top, war mace out, and floated straight toward him.

This is madness, Grey Cloak thought. He wasn't a mere

mortal with no power of his own. He was a natural, a Sky Rider. *Certainly I can do more than float here and die!*

Dyphestive spun right toward him. Grey Cloak ducked under the fierce swing that would have taken his head off.

Swish!

Tatiana fired an energy bolt from the Star of Light at Verbard. The silver-eyed underling created a small bloodred mystic shield with his free hand and knocked her bolt aside. With a flip of Catten's fingers, Tatiana was knocked head over heels and slammed into one of the archways.

"Finish off the one with the pointed ears, brother," Catten said. "I want to see him bleed."

"It will be my pleasure," Verbard replied. Guiding the spinning Dyphestive with his hand, he launched him in Grey Cloak's direction. "But I need you to hold the lithe one still."

"Not a problem," Catten boasted.

Grey Cloak felt an unseen force invade his body. His limbs stiffened like fence posts. Dyphestive was going to clobber him. *Noooooooooo!* He summoned wizard fire into his hands and blasted a shot out of his fingers into the floor. It propelled him above Dyphestive's lethal swing.

Swish!

"How creative. The one with polished features contains magic too. We'll find out how much after we rip him open,"

Catten said. He pointed at Grey Cloak. "But first a hard drop."

Grey Cloak's head almost touched the twenty-foot-high angled ceiling. Released by Verbard's power, he dropped into a sudden freefall that would break his bones. The Cloak of Legends billowed out, and he floated toward the ground. "A valiant try, fiends, but it will take more than —*ack!*"

A possessed, spinning Dyphestive crashed into him. His upper-right arm bone snapped against the full force of the war mace. Blinding pain lanced up his arm, through his neck, and into his eyes. Grey Cloak still made a soft landing on the floor, but Dyphestive crashed at his feet.

The young warrior sat up, shaking the cobwebs from his head. He gave Grey Cloak a guilty look. "I'm sorry."

"Forget about it." Grey Cloak jumped in front of his addled brother. He pulled the sword free from his belt and filled it with wizardry. The blade shone with glaring light.

The underlings squinted, shielded their eyes, and Catten said, "Oh no, he's going to blind us with his sword."

"His glowing sword," Verbard mocked.

"That very one."

"How dare he?" Verbard glared at Grey Cloak with eyes that could burn holes in metal. "I'm tired of this." His fingertips heated to a red-hot glow. "Let's finish them, brother. I'm ready to explore our new world."

"As you wish." With the helmet in one hand and lances of lightning in the other, Catten attacked.

Using the sword as a shield, Grey Cloak absorbed his all-powerful firepower, using the training Yuri Gnome-knower had put him through. He took everything that he could. The underling's firepower burned in his sword with a pulsating web of energy. He summoned all he had in him to push them back. "Aaaaaaaaaaaaah!"

Grey Cloak's fire burned brighter.

Dyphestive latched onto his wrists and joined him in another desperate howl. "Aaaaaaaaaaah!"

With a violent wave of their hands, the underlings snuffed Grey Cloak's wizardry out and sent the blood brothers sprawling to the floor.

Grey Cloak had nothing left. Dyphestive lay on his back, trembling. They watched helplessly as the underlings hovered over them with lances of fire in their hands, their countenances twisted with evil, ready to deliver the death blow.

Zooks.

21

Catten and Verbard glowered down at Grey Cloak and Dyphestive with murder in their metallic eyes. Tendrils of lightning fired out of their red-hot fingertips.

Grey Cloak and Dyphestive twitched and groaned on the floor in mighty spasms.

The underlings' fire sputtered out. They exchanged confused looks and tried to fire their mystic arrays again.

"What's amiss, brother?" Verbard asked with a disappointed hiss. His eyes widened as he studied his brother. "You fade. We fade! It will be the black tomb for us!"

Grey Cloak forced his way up to his elbows. "The visit is over, dung piles!" He wiggled his fingers. "Goodbye."

Catten swung his head around and set his eyes on the smoking Figurine of Heroes. It still stood in front of the flashing images of the time mural.

Grey Cloak read the underling's eyes instantly. He popped to his feet from the flat of his back, dashed for the figurine, and dove.

With a whisper of breath, Catten sent the Figurine of Heroes into the time mural. One image changed to another inside the ominous archway, and the figurine was lost forever.

Holding his broken arm, Grey Cloak turned and watched the underlings' bodies solidify with sheer evil glee on their faces.

"We've cheated death, brother," Verbard said. He shook his fists in the air. "Forever we will survive!"

"Yes," Catten said as his revived glowing fingertips needled the air. "And we have these rodents to thank for it. I'm feeling merciful. Let's kill them instantly." He cupped his hands together. "I can't wait to witness what lies beyond these walls. A new conquest in the making."

The underlings' hands radiated with new power. They sucked the air in hungrily through their small sharpened teeth.

Grey Cloak swallowed. He'd failed. None of this ever would have happened if he'd never used the figurine in the first place. Now, he'd set a new terror loose in the world, and it would never be the same.

He heard a voice in his head say, *Into the time mural. Run!*

At that moment, he watched Dyphestive rise to his feet.

He swayed like a punch-drunk boxer and faced the underlings. He lifted his war hammer up and beckoned the underlings to come forward.

With their eyes hungry for death, the underlings let their fire explode from their fingertips. A moment before the lightning cracked into Dyphestive's body, a new ally emerged.

Gossamer appeared from the wreckage of corpses. He stood behind the underlings with his silver-headed cane locked in both of his hands. Purple bands of energy encircled the underlings and constricted them like a great fire snake.

Catten and Verbard let out savage hisses as the coils burned through their robes and into their flesh. The dragon-charm helm slipped from Catten's grip and bounced on the floor.

"Go! Now!" Gossamer yelled at Dyphestive. "Into the time mural. It is your only choice!" He grimaced. "*Have faith!*"

Dyphestive lumbered on heavy feet toward Grey Cloak.

Streak took off and flew like a bird into Grey Cloak's arms.

Tatiana was on her feet again and turning the Star of Light loose on the underlings.

"Tatiana, come with us," Grey Cloak pleaded.

"I belong here. Be well. Be brave," she said as she and

Gossamer engaged the underlings in a battle of flame and fire.

Grey Cloak looked into the time mural's flashing array of images then back over his shoulder. "We can't leave them!"

The exchange of wizardly powers looked and sounded like the entire tower was going to erupt. Bright, scintillating light flashed in their eyes.

In a sudden move, Dyphestive caught Grey Cloak and Streak up in his crushing arms. "We'll take our chances." Without looking back, he thrust them all, body and soul, into the mural.

22

"Aaaaaaaaaaaaaaaaaaaaaaaaaaaaaaaaaaaaaaah!" Grey Cloak didn't know if he was screaming vocally or mentally. All he knew was that his spirit left his body and came back over and over again with the terrible sensation of falling to his doom.

There was no up. No down. He passed through air like water. He couldn't breathe. He spun through a tunnel of black-and-swirling colors. His past, present, and future soared by his eyes. He swam, but he did not fly.

The ground rushed up to greet him. "Ooooooof!" Grey Cloak found himself on his back, looking up just as Dyphestive came down. He jumped to one side.

Dyphestive landed inches from crushing him like a horse dropped out of the sky. A plume of dust went up from the youth's brawny body.

Grey Cloak rolled over on his broken arm and sucked air through his teeth. "Zooks," he muttered with the sun shining in his eyes. His stomach twisted inside his belly as he shielded his eyes and squinted.

Dyphestive pushed his face out of the dirt. "Are you hurt?"

"No thanks to you. You busted me in the arm with your hammer," Grey Cloak answered.

"I did?" Dyphestive rubbed the dust off his clothes. "I don't remember that. With this?" He held up the war mace.

"Yes, your hammer."

"Thunderash is a mace."

"Whatever it is, you about cracked my skull open with it. I suppose I should be thankful that you didn't and I only have a broken arm to show for it." Grey Cloak stood and did a full turn with the sandy ground crunching underfoot.

They were in a bleak stretch of land that showed nothing but leagues of brown brush and hard-packed earth in all directions. The air was dry, and the wavering heat rose from the ground in plumes. Trees stood, crooked and gnarled, their branches without a leaf on them. A dry riverbed with cattle bones snaked across the land nearby.

Dyphestive stood. "Sorry about your arm. I don't know what happened. I blacked out. I know I was spinning, but that was it."

"It happens," Grey Cloak said. His arm throbbed from

the pain. It was broken halfway between his elbow and shoulder. He needed to put a splint on it. "Gah!"

"What?" Dyphestive asked, his eyes widening.

Somehow, Streak had latched onto Grey Cloak's back, and he was crawling out from underneath Grey Cloak's cloak.

Grey Cloak took a knee and pet the dragon's head. "Someone sank his claws too deep, but I'll forgive him." He smiled at the dragon. "I'm glad you're well, boy."

"We better set that arm, or it'll get bad," Dyphestive said as he looked about. "I'll find some wood." He eyed his brother. "Do you have any idea where we are?"

Grey Cloak shook his head with grim eyes. "According to Gossamer, we could be at any time or place in Gapoli." He pinched some dust from the ground and let it fall. "It certainly isn't Arrowwood."

"Agreed." Dyphestive found a small dog tree nearby and began breaking off branches with his bare hands. Using a small knife that he possessed, he skinned the thin bark in long strips.

Much to Grey Cloak's surprise, Dyphestive created a sturdy splint around his arm. "Well done. Where'd you learn that?"

"The Doom Riders."

"Ah, I guess I shouldn't have asked."

"I don't mind." Dyphestive finished setting the splint. "Try not to move it. We'll have to find you some help in the meantime. Grey, do you think that Tatiana and Gossamer survived?"

No, he thought. The underlings would have killed them if they hadn't run, and it was his fault for using the figurine. He should have parted with it long ago, but he hadn't, and now more lives had been lost because of it. "I think it's best that we believe they survived and we have to find them."

Dyphestive eyed the distant sun that was beginning to set in the west. "North, then, until we learn where we are?"

"I'd say that's a wise idea." Together, he, Dyphestive, and Streak began their march northward. "If I were to venture a guess, I'd say that we're in Sulter Slay. We've been there before, if you remember."

"It feels like a lifetime ago," Dyphestive said as he plodded along with one arm swinging and the other arm hefting his war mace on his shoulder. "You know, there's a Wizard Watch in Sulter Slay."

"I certainly do." Grey Cloak managed a grim smile. They had traveled to the Wizard Watch in Sulter Slay when they'd first joined Talon. So many had died since then. Adanadel, Browning, and Dalsay were the first to die at the hands of the Doom Riders. They'd lost Grunt the minotaur too. Now Tatiana might be lost, as well as Gossamer. Death followed them everywhere, it seemed.

They moved at a brisk pace, league after league. There was no brook or stream to be found or so much as a shady tree to shield them from the sun beating down on their faces.

Dyphestive's vest and trousers were damp, and sweat dripped from his brow. The young juggernaut marched on, unfazed by the extreme weather.

Grey Cloak licked his dry lips. For a man who didn't eat or drink much, he was thirsty, more thirsty than he'd ever been. "A breeze would be nice."

Dyphestive grunted, while Streak scurried along like he couldn't be more at home. He chased small bugs and ate them.

"Marvelous," Grey Cloak said.

"What's that?" Dyphestive asked.

"I was thinking we might have to eat bugs. I never would've imagined," he said.

During his time with the Sky Riders, he had been trained on survival techniques. There had been a point where he was supposed to eat bugs to survive on a long outing. He'd refused, considering the act undignified for him, but this time, it was different.

Perhaps all of the excitement caught up with me. I'm starving.

"Are you really hungry?" Dyphestive asked. "I'm a little hungry, but I had some venison before we, well, left. You should have had some, but you never eat. That's not good for you."

"Well, today it isn't. That's for certain." He paused and took a knee. "Let's stop for a moment," he said.

Dyphestive tilted his head to one side and gave Grey Cloak a curious look. "You never stop."

"Well, I am now!" he shouted. Sweat dripped into his eye. He thumbed it away and took a breath. "Sorry, brother, but I don't feel like myself. I feel..." He fell face-first into the sand.

23

Dyphestive rushed over to Grey Cloak and rolled him over. His brother's face had red splotches all over it. He was clammy and covered in a cold sweat. He shook his brother gently. "Grey! Grey!"

Grey Cloak let out a raspy, dry-throated sigh that sounded like he was choking to death. His neck was limp, allowing his head to hang over one shoulder.

"Grey, what's wrong?" Dyphestive asked. He'd never seen his spry brother in such poor condition ever. He placed his hand on Grey Cloak's forehead. "You're burning up."

With no other recourse to consider, he stripped his brother down to his trousers. He fanned Grey Cloak with the Cloak of Legends and used his body to shield Grey Cloak from the sun.

Streak stood by Dyphestive's side, tongue flickering out of his mouth. He nudged Grey Cloak with his snout several times.

Kneeling, Dyphestive said, "I don't know what happened. Perhaps the heat drained him. He needs water. Can you find water, Streak?"

Streak bunched his back legs and launched himself into the sky. He flew like a chubby featherless bird through the air with his stout tail hanging behind him.

The red splotches covered Grey Cloak's wiry frame like giant freckles.

Dyphestive had seen sickness before, including heat exhaustion, back at Rhonna's farm. But he'd never seen anything like Grey Cloak's rash. "I don't know what to do, Grey. I don't know." His thick fingers fumbled and poked over Grey Cloak's rigid body. He even put his ear to his brother's chest and listed to his breathing and heartbeat. Both were shallow and weak.

He fanned Grey Cloak with his cloak and watched the splotches spread. Grey Cloak spasmed.

"Nooooo," Dyphestive moaned as he clutched at the hairs on his head. "Noooo."

Grey Cloak rolled over on his good arm as he foamed at the mouth, kicked, and spasmed. He fell forward on his belly.

That was when Dyphestive saw it. A strange creature had fastened itself to the lower middle of Grey Cloak's back. It looked like a spotted red crab the size of a small hand. Its legs and pincers were deep in Grey Cloak's skin. Its shell was translucent, and blood flowed through it as it pulsed.

Dyphestive swallowed the lump building in his throat. The sickening tick of a creature grew as it filled with blood. He grabbed the thing in his hand and tried to rip it out.

Grey Cloak let out a shriek.

Dyphestive let go the blood-sucking creature. "What do I do?" He wiped the sweat from his brow with his forearm. "Grey Cloak, what do I do?" He eyed the sky, searching for Streak. He needed help, and he needed it now.

Grey Cloak spasmed and spit out more foam. He looked awful. His vibrant skin was pale, and his mouth hung open.

Dyphestive pulled his knife and decided to cut the nasty insect off. It continued to enlarge as it filled with blood, and the hump on its back bulged. He brought the knife's tip to the blood sac and prepared to poke it.

"I wouldn't do that," someone said.

Dyphestive's head twisted around to face a dwarf with sandy-brown hair, a beard tied into a bun below his chin, and sun-browned skin. The dwarf wore desert robes, and he had cold blue eyes. He carried a gnarled wooden staff as tall as him. "Who are you?"

"Your only hope to save him," the dwarf said in a gravelly voice. He looked down at Grey Cloak. His eyes had deep crow's feet, and his hands were leathery. "Your friend was bitten by a desert blood tick. Very rare and fatal. I'm surprised your friend still lives."

"Can you really help him?" Dyphestive asked.

The dwarf eyed Thunderash, which was lying nearby. He rubbed his chin. "For a price." He tapped his staff on the ground two times. "Pick him up, and come with me. We have a very long walk."

Dyphestive put his knife away and did as he was told. He knew very little about dwarves, aside from Rhonna. They weren't like the other races that galivanted about Gapoli like the others. They were more secluded in the south, crafty, unpredictable, and self-serving. Rhonna had shared that much about her people.

"Come," the dwarf said, heading west.

"I-uh..." He scanned the skies.

"I know. You have a dragon. He'll find us. Come. It's a long journey." The dwarf moved at a brisk pace on his stubby legs. "I'm Koll, a druid, if you must know. You're fortunate that I came upon your tracks and fortunate that I am nosy." He thumbed his big snout. "I found your tracks strange."

Holding Grey Cloak in his arms, Dyphestive asked, "You found what strange?"

"Your tracks. Your tracks started in the middle of nowhere. How does that happen?" Koll asked. "Did you fall out of the sky? I've seen stars fall but not men."

"It's a long story." Grey Cloak was as warm as toast in his arms. Dyphestive could see two waterskins that Koll carried. "Do you have water? He's burning up."

"No. Water won't help him either," Koll said as he loosened his waterskin and took a drink. He capped the waterskin without offering any to Dyphestive. "It'll take more than that to save him. Tell me more about how you came here."

"Only if you give my friend a drink."

Koll stopped at a rise among the rocks and tapped his staff twice. "This is my water. Get your own." He turned and walked on.

24

"I can't really explain it. It's called a time mural. We jumped through it and landed here," Dyphestive said.

"Landed on a desert blood tick is what you did. Ignorant thing to do," Koll said. The dwarf never stopped walking west along the winding dusty trails of the south. "Very stupid."

"We didn't have any choice of where we landed," Dyphestive commented. While carrying Grey Cloak in his arms, he'd been telling Koll parts of their journey minus many details. He'd gotten better about keeping his mouth shut over the years, even though it was in his nature to be completely honest. "What would you have done? Those underlings were going to kill us, and well, we didn't have a choice."

"A dwarf would have fought with his last drop of

blood," Koll said. He looked back at Dyphestive and wiggled his bushy eyebrows. "Huh, I would have done the same thing, I suppose. I'm no dwarven warrior. I'm a druid, dedicated to knowledge about nature. It will get cold soon, dangerous."

"How are we going to help my friend?" Dyphestive asked. "All we've been doing is walking. Don't you have a village?"

"Village? Hack! Druids don't live in villages. This is where I live." Koll stooped over a small round cactus bush. With his bare hands, he ripped the top off. "You said you wanted water. Drink."

"I didn't want it. I wanted it for my friend." Dyphestive helped himself to the small watery pulps inside the cactus. He squeezed water over Grey Cloak's lips and head. "He feels like he's on fire."

Koll eyed the stars appearing in the sky. "You share strange tales, very strange indeed. I've wandered Dwarf Skull all my life, most of Sulter Slay. I've never been anywhere else. What you say is... entertaining."

"I'm glad you're amused." Dyphestive rolled Grey Cloak over and looked at the desert blood tick. It had blown up to half the size of his hand. "Horseshoes! It's getting worse. How much can this thing drink? Won't it let go?"

"Not until it's finished," Koll said. He tapped his staff twice. "We need to find shelter. In the night are many prowlers. They'll smell our blood. It's too hot to hunt in the day, but in the night, if they find our scent, they will come."

"Won't a fire keep them away?"

"Fire will attract them." Koll wandered over to Grey Cloak and held his wrist. "Your friend is strong. I'm very surprised he breathes. Impressive." He sucked down fluid from his waterskin. "You want to remove the tick, but if you do, it will inject more poison. Poison paralyzes your friend now. Rattle the insect, and it will kill him. Come."

The trek continued upward into the rocky terrain that zigzagged higher and higher. Grey Cloak wasn't particularly heavy, but after such a long walk, even Dyphestive's mighty shoulders started to burn.

I won't let you down, Grey. Hang on.

"If you don't have a village, then where are you taking us? Is there another village with people who can help?" he asked.

"Why do you think dwarves live in villages? Dwarves don't live in huts. They live in buildings, cottages, fortresses, structures. Don't ever call a dwarven home a village, or a hut. It's an insult, not that it matters to me." Koll hustled over some broken stones and vanished on the other side.

Taking long steps, Dyphestive climbed over the rocks, trying to catch up with the dwarf. They were high up in the hills overlooking the sun-cracked plains. The sun had fully set, and the plains had darkened to a black sea. He lost sight of Koll and didn't hear so much as a scuffle.

"Koll," he called out.

"Hush, young fool," Koll said quietly. He'd gathered himself in a cluster of rocks and blended right in. "Come. Look."

Koll was pointing his staff down toward the plains. Keeping his voice low, he said, "Do you see that?"

Dyphestive narrowed his eyes. He saw only blackness at first, but as his vision adjusted, bright spots, like fireflies, appeared in the dark. "Are those torches?"

"Yes," Koll said. He sucked his teeth. "We're being followed."

"By who?"

"Scavengers, most likely. I hoped to avoid them, but they're thick in this barren wood." Koll kept his eyes fixed on the train of torchlight. "There are only three torches, but don't be fooled. That is only the smaller part of a much larger pack."

"Is it stupid of me to ask what the Scavengers are?"

"An assortment of bloodthirsty nomads. They prey on people and kill as they please. As long as they don't interfere with Dwarf Skull's affairs, they are left in peace." Koll hopped down from his hiding spot. "We need to move faster. If they don't catch us by daybreak, they'll leave us be. And the hill rock should slow them down. Let's move. Quickly."

"You never said who the Scavengers were. Are they orcs, goblins, gnolls, *dwarves*?" Dyphestive asked.

"I said they were an assortment. Pray you don't have to see them for yourself. If you do, you'll be too close, and they'll skin you alive." Koll eyed Grey Cloak's limp form. "And him, dead or alive."

Dyphestive hustled after Koll with a lot of questions on his mind. "Why would they kill us? Wouldn't they rob us?"

"Think about it, boy. Did you see fields of farmland and cattle out here? Why else would they hunt the living? Huh?"

"They'll eat us?"

"You aren't as dull as you look, but that took some time. Yes, they will eat us, just like a buzzard that picks away at exhausted flesh." Koll tapped his staff. "They'll use the marrow of our bones to flavor their soup, and you'll watch while they do it."

25

K oll led them on a brutal trek through the rugged hills. His feet were as sure as a mountain goat's, but Dyphestive's weren't. With Grey Cloak on his shoulder, he slipped more than once on the loose rock and cracked his knees. He pressed on.

"I know a spot, a refuge. We can hide there. It's close," Koll said as he drank from his waterskin. He offered it to Dyphestive. "Drink, big fella. There's no sense in being stingy now."

The skin didn't have much water left, but he wet Grey Cloak's lips the best he could and squeezed the remainder into his mouth.

Meanwhile, the surefooted Koll climbed up on the crag. He wasn't up there long before he scrambled back down. "I can see the flicker of their torches. They aren't so far off as I'd hoped. They move quick. Come."

For hours, they snaked their way through the black hills as fast as their legs could take them. It was dark, slippery, and difficult to navigate in many spots, with gullies that needed to be jumped and rises that needed to be climbed. Dyphestive fought his way through all of it. It was even harder with an elf on his shoulder. He used his war mace as a cane on many occasions.

"I don't think we'll make it to tomorrow," Koll commented as they moved onward. "It's hours until dawn, and they won't slow until late morning. I know spots in these hills, good ones. We'll hide in one and wait it out. So long as the basilisks don't sniff us out, we should be fine."

"What about Streak?" Dyphestive asked. "How will he find us?"

"Your dragon? I'm certain he's safer than we are. Be thankful."

They traveled another hour or so until Koll led them into a large burrow nestled in the rocks. It was covered by prickly overgrowth.

Dyphestive slunk underneath the wild brush and duck-walked inside. The burrow was large, more like a cave, and many yards deep. He heard Koll's sandals scuffling over the ground. He followed the dwarf deeper until he bumped into him. "Sorry."

"This is as deep as we go. Now, we wait but first—" Koll crawled by him. "A trick."

Even though it was pitch-black, Dyphestive could make out Koll's rugged form crawling toward the burrow's end. Koll started to chant and mutter in gibberish. Dyphestive's arm hairs stood on end.

At the end of the cave, shades of moonlight bled through the prickly brush. The tangles of vines and thorns grew longer and thicker.

Koll crawled back. "I told you I'm a druid. I have tricks, tricks that have fooled the Scavengers many times. They know me, but they have not caught me." He cleared his throat. "Now, make yourself comfortable, and be quiet. Get some rest, perhaps. I'll stand watch. I sleep little."

"You sound like my friend. This is the most he's ever slept."

"Hush now."

Dyphestive breathed deeply through his nostrils. It had been a long and crazy journey that had started halfway across the world. Now, he found himself in Sulter Slay, trusting a dwarf druid he'd just met, and was being chased by flesh-hungry nomads called Scavengers. To make matters worse, Grey Cloak was down-and-out. Dyphestive was desperate to help him.

And Streak is gone too. If Grey wakes up, he'll kill me. Horse-shoes, I don't even know what I'm running from. I bet I could handle whatever's after us. I'll use Thunderash and bash their skulls in. He would rather fight his way out than anything, but Grey Cloak's breathing was shallow. He wouldn't risk Grey Cloak getting hurt or captured, so he waited.

I feel like a bear in his den. He shifted his shoulders, trying to make more room, but there wasn't any. *This is awful.*

"Relax, young fella," Koll whispered. "Trust the night to see us through."

Dyphestive could have sworn that Koll started to hum. It was an easy, earthy tune, and his eyelids became very heavy and closed.

SOMETHING KICKED DYPHESTIVE'S LEG. His eyes opened, and he realized that Grey Cloak had booted him during a spasm. He stretched his head up and bumped into the ceiling. Dirt fell into his hair. He brushed out the dirt and noticed daylight creeping through the brush that covered the burrow. He also noticed that Koll was gone.

"Huh." Leaving Grey Cloak, his war mace in hand, he crawled on hands and knees toward the end of the cave. The thorny brush had been pushed open. He stopped and listened. The morning winds in the high hills whistled through the rocks with haunting effect. He poked his head out into the glare of the sun. He immediately felt the morning heat on his neck. The sun was rising in the east.

He pushed out of the burrow in between the wedges of sandy rock.

There was no sign of Koll.

He must be scouting.

Staying low, Dyphestive crawled out of the rocks to a higher elevation. He could see for leagues all around, but there was no sign of the dwarven druid.

Did he abandon me?

He knew nothing of Koll, and it wouldn't surprise him one bit if the dwarf had fled. But Koll was the only guide he had in the barren land. Hidden behind the rock, Dyphestive studied the surrounding plains. He saw no sign of a single soul in any direction. The only living thing was him and the wind.

The hairs on the back of his neck stood up. He closed his eyes and listened. Something scraped over the rocks behind the next rise. A clicking sound came with it. He turned just as a huge lizard head appeared over the rocks. It was a basilisk with a round head like a snake, thousands of sharp tiny teeth, and a black tongue that licked the rock. It was big enough to ride, complete with a harness, but no one rode on its back.

The basilisk fixed its bright-yellow eyes on Dyphestive. Head low, dripping jaws open, it scrabbled over the rocks on a collision course with him.

26

Dyphestive hit the giant lizard on the top of the nose with a bone-cracking blow. It didn't stop the lizard from plowing him over. They tumbled down the rocks and over the hillside. He found himself on the bottom of the pile. He had Thunderash stuffed in the basilisk's jaws, keeping its thousands of teeth at bay.

He shoved the monster back and set his legs underneath it. It was the size of a horse and just as heavy. Stuffing his boots in its belly, he pushed.

The basilisk flopped on its side but not without a prize. It tore the war mace out of Dyphestive's fingertips as it rolled over, twisted on the ground, and came to its feet. It charged again.

Weaponless, Dyphestive's large hands instinctively pulled out his knife. He let out an angry growl and charged.

He and the giant lizard collided. He brought the dagger down into its serpentine skin and aimed for its eyeball. Steel sank hilt deep into the soft tissue that made up the lizard's eye.

The lizard swung its entire body around and flattened Dyphestive as he continued to stab. He rolled up on all fours and watched the basilisk shake its thick neck and teeter.

Lungs burning, Dyphestive rushed it again. "Raaaaaaah!" He jumped over its snapping jaws and landed on the monster's back. He punched the knife deep into the monster's neck with mighty blows. It gushed blood, and its legs quivered.

The basilisk staggered over the dusty ground. Its feet faltered beneath it as it stumbled and fell.

Dyphestive tore the war mace out of the dying monster's jaws. He filled his lungs with air and let out a gusty breath. The basilisk was dead, but it wore a leather harness made by men. On pins and needles, he resumed his search for Koll.

The search ended quickly as he spied a group of men on the trail. A dozen men of various sizes in desert garb with cowls wrapped around their heads approached him. They wore sword belts on their hips and packs on their backs. Even though their heads were covered, he could see the heavy stares underneath. He recognized one of them, the shortest one in the group, Koll. The dwarven druid's hands were bound behind his back, and he was being dragged down the trail by a rope.

Dyphestive held Thunderash in a white-knuckled grip and cocked it over his shoulder. "If you know what's best for you, you'll let him go and walk away."

The hard-eyed Scavengers stopped twenty feet away. Vultures circled in the sky above.

Koll's beard was full of grit. He rolled to his side. "I'm sorry, Dyphestive." He spat. "I went to scout, and they caught me."

"No need to apologize." He gave the group a hard look. They weren't Monarch Knights or Honor Guards. That much was certain. They carried weapons but wore no visible armor. Their gear wasn't the finest craft either. Their swords were notched, and the tips of their daggers broken. One of them was really big, though, bigger than Dyphestive, and more of them could be close by. He pulled the war mace off his shoulder and tapped it into his hand. "Last warning. Let him go, or I'll do worse to you than I did that lizard."

One of the Scavengers moved behind Koll. He had a rangy build and bright-green eyes. He pulled a curved dagger with wooden finger grips from his belt. He lifted Koll up by the hair and put the dagger to his neck. In a dry voice, he said, "Surrender, or he dies, fool."

Dyphestive swallowed. He was ready to brawl, not

negotiate. His gut told him to fight, but the pleading look in Koll's eyes suggested otherwise.

"You don't need to save me, boy," Koll said. "I've lived long enough. Save yourself. I'll be better off in the dwarven mountains of the dead."

With a flip of his war mace, Dyphestive said, "Perhaps we can negotiate. I'll give you all that I have. This war mace is worth more than all that you possess, and it's magic. Take it."

"You killed our basilisk," the Scavenger with the dagger said.

"How much can a lizard be worth?" he replied. He had no idea how much a basilisk was worth. "This could buy ten of them. Twenty!"

The leader pressed the dagger harder against Koll's beard. "Surrender, or he dies. I won't ask again." He gave Dyphestive a warning look. "Drop the weapon."

Dyphestive spun the weapon around one more time, and with a defeated look, he let it slip through his fingers. If Koll weren't in danger, he would have fought them all. Something told him that he could beat them.

"Secure him," the lead Scavenger said as he pulled the knife away from Koll and slipped it into his belt. "Make the bonds tight. He's a strong one."

Two Scavengers slipped in behind Dyphestive and bound his arms behind his back with cords of leather. The cords bit deep into his skin as they looped them around his thick wrists more than once. They patted him down, took away his knife, and stripped him down to his vest, boots, and trousers. With a shove, they put him on his knees.

"Better," the leader said. He bent over and sawed away the cords that bound Koll's hands behind his back.

Dyphestive's heart sank.

Koll gave a wry smile and rubbed his wrists. "You should have trusted your instincts, young fella." He looked at the leader. "Fetch the other one in the cave, and keep an eye out for their dragon."

27

Traveling became a bitter event over the sun-cracked ground of Sulter Slay. Dyphestive was tied to a basilisk, and so was Grey Cloak. In a cruel twist, Grey Cloak was towed behind the lizard like a log.

Dyphestive pleaded with the Scavengers to let him carry his friend. The coldhearted Scavengers cut off his requests by whacking him all over with clubs. He clammed up after the third time, instead opting to play along while casually looking skyward for Streak. The little dragon might be the only hope they had.

Koll took a moment to fall back from the pack and join him. The dwarf didn't seem chipper like he had been before. Instead, he seemed cold and calculating. "Don't feel bad, young man. Men and women more seasoned than you have fallen prey to our traps. I've been doing this a long time. I'm very good at it. Huh."

Dyphestive clenched his jaw. If he ever got his hands on the dwarf, he would break his neck.

"You may speak." He tapped his staff twice on the ground. "The Scavengers won't throttle you as long as you're spoken to first."

Hearing the dwarf's confident tone, Dyphestive decided to play the role of the fearful and downtrodden. *Let them think I'm young and stupid. Get the dwarf talking.* "Are you really going to eat us?"

"Perhaps," Koll said. "We can find many uses for men like you."

Dyphestive purposefully stumbled on a stone and fell to his knees.

The Scavengers stopped and turned.

He scrambled up, and with a worried look, he said, "I'm sorry. I'm sorry." He huffed for breath. "What else would you do with us?"

"That will be decided later."

Dyphestive looked back at Grey Cloak. "Is he going to die from the tick bite?"

"He will if we don't take it off, but for now, it's a foolproof way to keep him incapacitated." Koll fingered his beard shaped like a bun. "We are fortunate that he fell upon it. You might have been more formidable otherwise."

Keep him talking, Dyphestive thought. Koll had given

him a hint that the tick might not be as fatal as it seemed, and they were concerned about numbers. It seemed that the Scavengers wouldn't take on a strong group, at least not without numbers. At the present, there were only twelve Scavengers plus Koll. Three of them rode giant lizards.

If I had a suit of armor, I think I could take them. The problem was he didn't have a suit of armor, and he couldn't put Grey Cloak in danger. If he tried anything, they could kill Grey Cloak.

Dyphestive subtly strained against his bonds. His wrists were wrapped so tightly that he couldn't feel his fingers. He imagined them being bloodred. Without any sort of leverage, he had little hope of breaking them.

"Do we have far?" he asked.

"Why, are you in a hurry to die?" Koll replied.

"No."

A DAY LATER, shortly after nightfall came, the Scavengers arrived at a small fortress in the hills long eroded by time. The rocks that made up its foundation still stood, but half of the walls had fallen, leaving gaps around the building. The group sauntered inside, where a large fire burned in the center courtyard.

Women and children with tattooed faces rushed out to greet the men. They were human, orcen, and a mix of the two. All of them looked hard and durable. Within moments, the children were hurling rocks at Dyphestive until Koll and a pair of Scavengers chased them away.

Dyphestive was led into a man-size metal cage, and Grey Cloak was placed in another. They were positioned near one of the walls that was still standing, and he had a full view of the fire, where the Scavengers victoriously gathered.

Koll wandered over after Dyphestive and Grey Cloak were situated. A lone Scavenger with a full battle array that consisted of a short curved sword, a pair of daggers, and a spear came with him. "Don't get jumpy, or my man will skewer you."

Giving the dwarf a heavy look, Dyphestive said, "I thought you were going to skewer me anyway."

"We will hold a council about that, but first we will celebrate," Koll said as he searched Dyphestive's eyes. "Mind yourself, and we'll feed you."

"You keep strange company for a dwarf, don't you?" Dyphestive asked.

"Why do you say that?"

Dyphestive leaned over and looked beyond Koll. "I don't see any other dwarves. I thought dwarves were clannish. Dwarven pride."

"That's not a life for everyone," Koll replied. He looked at Grey Cloak. "He's strong for an elf, but as you can see, his cheeks are sinking. He might make it through the morning, or he might not."

"You have to help him!" Dyphestive demanded. "You said you can."

The Scavenger thrust his spear in Dyphestive's face.

"We will hold a council about it but not until after we celebrate. It's custom." Koll rapped his short staff twice on the cage. "Be wise, and rest. Forget about your friend. His life is not in your hands but ours." He walked away.

The celebration began with the Scavengers dancing wildly around the bonfire. The women flung their bodies into the arms of their men, danced, and cavorted provocatively. They seemed to feel no shame as they peeled off the men's cowls as part of the ceremonial dance.

Like the women and children, the men had colorful tattoos and piercings all over their faces. Their expressions were savage and fierce, and the craftiness of evil men lingered in their eyes.

Dyphestive felt his guts twist the more he watched. He'd never seen men and women act so foul. They smoked from pipes and danced in heated passion. The children joined along in the dark and savage songs. They beat the leather heads of drums.

And I thought it was bad in Dark Mountain. At least there was some decorum.

The Scavenger men jumped and let out shrill screams with children on their shoulders. The women showered

Koll with haughty affection as they layered him with wreaths of tiny bones. On and on it went in foul celebration as they praised the sky above them and the ground beneath their feet.

Earlier, Dyphestive had thought Koll had in mind a prolonged servitude as a slave for his imprisonment. That would have given him time to plan an escape, but it was clear that whatever they had in mind would be an act of torment and pure evil.

No matter the cost, I have to escape.

28

The Scavengers held hands and danced around the bonfire, chortling with wicked glee. The women's shrieking voices reached a feverish pitch as the men hollered louder and louder.

Women in snug leather skirts strutted toward the blaze and tossed a sandy substance into the fire, which swallowed it up and spit out bright-colored flames. The pyre heaved and moaned like a living thing, feeding on the cold air and growing bigger.

From his uncomfortable position in the back of his pen, Dyphestive leaned forward. Figures twisted inside the flames. The muscles in his back knotted. He broke out in a cold sweat.

A supernatural event was happening, a demon or spirit from another world being summoned.

He saw Koll talking to two Scavengers and pointing at the cages. The Scavengers were towering brutes that had been part of the pack that had captured Dyphestive. They were full-blooded orcs with beady eyes, protruding foreheads, broad noses, and canine teeth. They hustled over to the holding pens, grabbed the ropes tied to Grey Cloak's cage, and dragged them toward the fire.

The Scavengers parted into two rows and chanted for the blood of the fallen elf. Dyphestive watched in horror as the six-foot-high cage was hauled forward by the two rows of chanting people. At the end of the row, before the fire, Koll waited with his staff over his head. His eyes were as bright as flames, and he chanted strange words.

Dyphestive's jaw hung open, and his heart raced as he watched Grey Cloak be pulled toward the hungry flames. *They're going to sacrifice him.*

The bonfire's flames stretched out over the crowd like great arms with long fingers. With haunting effect, the fires swayed through the air. In the center of the fire, at the top, was a head with a face. A burning elemental creature that had been summoned lived inside.

Dyphestive's mind screamed, *Noooooooooooo!*

The brutes unlocked Grey Cloak's cage and hauled him outside. They raised him high in the air for all to see.

The Scavengers erupted with cheers. The hammering of drums grew louder.

I must stop this!

With his blood surging through his veins, Dyphestive strained against the leather cords that bound him. As mighty as his strength was, they flexed but would not give. His hands were so big that he couldn't pull them free.

No! Think! What would Grey Cloak do?

He caught the guard giving him a backward glance. He discontinued his struggles until the guard turned away again. An idea came to him. It was something he'd seen Grey Cloak do before. Instead of breaking his bonds, he found a way to use them.

With his hands behind his back, he pushed them down to the ground and slid them underneath his rump. From there, he brought his hands under his knees. At that point, he was bunched up so tight, he could barely move. His big body didn't make it any easier. He wasn't a little man who could squirm out of tight situations, but given his youth, he was still flexible. Just enough, he hoped.

Almost there. You can do this.

Dyphestive tucked his chin into his chest, pulled his knees in as far as he could, and pushed his hands toward his ankles. The heels of his boots stopped him from freedom.

No. No. No. So close. Do it. Do it or die, Dyphestive!

With his body trembling, he stretched his arms out and heaved. The knots slipped over the heels of his boots, and he brought them over his toes.

I'm free!

He set his eyes on the guard who stood with his back toward Dyphestive. Without hesitation, he got to his feet and thrust his hands through the bars. He grabbed the man's hair and yanked him back. Before the man could cry out for help, Dyphestive trapped the man's neck in his bound wrists and choked the life out of him.

At the bonfire, Grey Cloak was lifted higher in the air and carried toward the flames. At the forefront, Koll chanted louder. The flames and the figure in the fire roared.

Dyphestive reached for the dead guard's dagger, whisked it out, and cut his bonds. He searched the guard's body for a key, but he couldn't find one.

"No, no, no, no, no!" He glanced up at the throng. So in the heat of passion they were, they didn't pay him any mind. He grabbed the bars and pulled. The thick metal groaned and began to bend. Biceps bulging, he pulled the bars back until one bar kissed the inside of another. He did the same to the other bar, creating a gap for him to squeeze his shoulders through.

Even with the rods bent, he didn't have enough space to squirm in between. He made it halfway out and got wedged in the bars. *Not good. I'm stuck.*

29

Dyphestive pushed himself back into the cage. He stripped off his vest and tried to squeeze through again. His sweat-slick frame slipped in between the bars. Pushing off with his feet, he popped through.

Freedom. The air tasted sweeter on the other side of the bars.

Grey Cloak's body was only a few feet from the flames. The fire elemental's hands reached out for him.

Dyphestive leaned over and scooped up the guard's spear. From over one hundred feet away, he hurled it toward the clamoring crowd.

The spear sailed silently through the darkness in a perfect arc. It came down and lanced one of the Scavenger brutes holding Grey Cloak through the heart. The orcen

Scavenger dropped dead, and Grey Cloak's body fell to the ground.

Dyphestive picked up a sword and dagger as the Scavengers fell silent and turned his way.

"Remember me?" Dyphestive growled. He banged his weapons together. "Because here I am."

Koll strutted to the front of the pack, pointed his staff at Dyphestive, and said with a raised voice, "Kill him!"

The Scavengers, one and all, snatched up their weapons and charged like a hungry pack of wolves. They outnumbered Dyphestive by more than twenty-five to one and came with glazed-over eyes.

He didn't care. They couldn't fight like him, and he was going to prove it. Bare chested, he charged, shouting, "For Grey Cloak!"

"ROOOOOOOOOOAAAAAAAAAAAARR!"

The Scavengers stopped in their tracks and collided with one another. They cowered and searched for the source of the frightening sound erupting in the sky.

"ROOOOOOOOOOAAAAAAAAAAAARR!"

Dyphestive knew that sound, and he didn't stop his charge. It was Streak. Before the first Scavenger he reached could turn to face him, he took the Scavenger's head off with his sword. A punch with his dagger dropped another Scavenger dead.

The women and children were the first to scatter as

they snatched the young ones up in their arms and hustled them away.

The men were far from as fortunate. Streak glided down from the sky, spitting flames. The Scavengers' clothing caught fire, and their skin burned as flames engulfed the evil men.

Dyphestive showed no mercy on the confused brood. His massive arms became windmills, his steel pumping out a bloody death. Scavengers were skewered and gored. They caught the full onslaught of Dyphestive's fury.

Out of the smoke and flame, one of the towering orcs came wielding Thunderash. He charged Dyphestive and swung with great force. Dyphestive blocked the war mace with the blade of his sword. The sword snapped like a dry branch. Without pause, the orcen Scavenger brought Thunderash down.

Dyphestive seized the orc by the wrists, and they shuffled back and forth over the dusty ground. The orc was strong, his limbs as hard as tree roots. He had a lot of fight in him as they wrestled to break one another's grip.

The orc headbutted Dyphestive with his thick skull. Dyphestive sneered and headbutted him back. *Crack.* He busted the orc's nose.

The orc lunged forward. They collided skull to skull and battered one another like rams.

"No one's skull is harder than mine," the orc boasted.

Crack. Crack. Crack.

The orc's knees buckled. His grip on the war mace failed. He swayed, blinked his eyes, and staggered back woozily. He rubbed his head. "Your skull is like iron." A dead body tripped him up, and he fell backward into the heap.

Dyphestive picked up his mace and finished the orc.

Streak soared in the sky, scattering the Scavengers with his flames. They burned and ran. They burned and died.

Dyphestive sought Koll out. The wicked dwarf had set him up and deceived him. He wouldn't let that happen to anyone ever again. Scanning the fort's grounds, he spied the dwarven druid cowering behind the women and children. "Koll! You're mine!"

The women and children ran for their lives.

Koll ran, too, but he wasn't fast enough to escape Dyphestive. At the last second, he spun around and swung his staff into Dyphestive's chest. The blow clapped like thunder. Dyphestive was knocked from his feet and lay flat on his back.

"You should have been wiser than to pursue an old dwarf," Koll said as he lorded over Dyphestive's fallen body. "Now I will feed you to the flames along with your friend. That is the price of vengeance." He lifted his staff, bringing it down with one final and fatal blow.

Dyphestive sat up, grimacing. He snatched Koll's staff, ripped it out of his grip, and flung it away. "Sticks and stones can't break my bones." He seized Koll by the neck. "But I can break yours!"

"No!" Koll shouted in outrage. "Impossible! I struck you down! I struck you down!"

Dyphestive hauled Koll, kicking and screaming, toward the burning and heaving fire. "Hungry?" he asked the elemental figure dancing in the flames. "How about some dwarf for dinner?" Dyphestive hurled Koll end over end into the bonfire. He dusted off his hands and walked away.

The women and children were nowhere in sight.

Every man he and Streak had fought was dead. Bodies burned on the ground. Whatever Streak could burn, he'd burned.

Dyphestive picked up Grey Cloak in his arms and grabbed his mace as well. He surveyed the fort and spoke with a booming voice. "I know you're out there. I know you see me, wicked people. Change your ways, or the same end will come to you!"

Without looking back, he walked out of the fort, leaving the smoke, flames, and death behind him. Following the stars, he resumed his journey north across the black landscape, ready to face any danger he must to save his friend.

30

His legs feeling like anchors, Dyphestive dropped to his knees and set Grey Cloak down. Even his inhuman endurance and strength wasn't enough to take his friend another step. The sun had baked him alive, and his skin was burned red. He licked his cracked lips.

The sun had set on him three times since he'd started walking, and he'd never crossed paths with another soul. He was in the middle of nowhere, and nowhere owned him.

If he fared badly, Grey Cloak didn't fare any better. The elf was still as pale as a sheet, but the clamminess was gone. He breathed in ragged sighs.

Streak landed beside the blood brothers. He studied Grey Cloak with probing eyes and licked the elf's fingers. The runt dragon had been flying off and on for the duration of the journey, flying out of sight before returning hours later. He came back with dead ground lizards, but even Dyphestive couldn't stomach the creatures.

With the sun beating down on his neck, he took a look at Grey Cloak's back. His stomach soured. The desert blood tick was bigger than his fist. Blue veins spidered along Grey Cloak's back in a weblike pattern from where the tick had sunk its pincers in.

Dyphestive dared to touch the blood sac bulging on the tick's back. Grey Cloak stiffened and gasped.

"Horseshoes." He took a breath and eyed the sky. There wasn't a cloud in sight, and there hadn't been for days. All he could do was walk north, but even then, he was uncertain as to where he was. Something felt amiss, and he hadn't drank a drop in days.

"Streak," he said with a dry throat. "If you can find help, find it. I can't go any farther. I'll stay with Grey Cloak."

The runt dragon cocked his head.

Dyphestive shooed the dragon away. "You must go, Streak. Go. I know you can do it."

Streak slunk beside Grey Cloak, licked his face, opened his wings, and flew away.

It took a lot of energy for Dyphestive to lift his head and watch the dragon vanish into the bright sky. Dizziness assailed him, and his vision filled with spots. He flopped face-first onto the desert sand.

DYPHESTIVE OPENED his eyes and found a sea of stars above him. He was moving but not by his own power. He was flat on his back, and a wagon was rolling beneath him, or so he thought.

It was all he could do to keep his eyes open. His limbs were exhausted, and he couldn't move them. Something restrained them. He flexed in a vain effort. He was too weak to fight.

The steady rhythm of the wagon rocking and rolling put him back to sleep.

"WAKEY, WAKEY," someone said.

Dyphestive felt someone tickling his nose with a feather. His eyes cracked open, and he stared at a little man with an impish face. He waved a turkey feather above him. "Ah, you see me, no?"

"Uh..." was all Dyphestive managed to say. It felt like his throat had swollen closed.

The little man with an impish face looked like a gnome. He had fox-like features that gave his face a curious expression. His mouth was big, his eyes slanted, and his nose came to a point. "You breathe. A good thing for you."

The gnome held out a clay jug. "This is water. Drink."

He poured it all over Dyphestive's face. "Good, no?" He giggled. "Try not to move. Your skin is peeling, and motion will be very painful, but we shall restore you."

Dyphestive forced himself into a sitting position. His back burned like it was going to split open when he did.

"No, no, no, you should lie down. I have salve. Lie down," the gnome said. He behaved with childlike manners as he patted Dyphestive's forearm. "Rest, rest."

Dyphestive swung his legs off the small cot. "I have a feeling I've been on my back long enough." He spied the room. It was a primitive cottage made out of packed mud walls and branches. The roof was held up by driftwood posts, and the ceiling wasn't very high. The cottage had no door but rather a doorway covered by a heavy blanket. Two steps led down into the main floor, which had been dug out. That was where he sat. It had cupboards and a small table and chairs. The floor was made of tight bundles of grass. He rubbed his feet on the grass. "Where are my boots?"

"Outside," the gnome said, pinching his nose. "They stank very bad. Don't you hurt? Your skin blisters."

"I'll manage." Grey Cloak lay on his chest on a cot in the middle of the floor. He was shirtless, and the desert blood tick was still fastened to his back. Grey Cloak's white and veiny skin looked awful. "Is he going to make it?"

"He breathes," the gnome said as he strutted around in a tattered vest, blue trousers, and bare feet. "I'll try to keep him breathing, but that blood tick has been on him a while."

"What's your name?"

The gnome's face brightened. "I'm Chopper. Friend of the desert, they call me. I've lived here all my life, and I know the ways, the creatures. I can tell one grain of sand apart from the other. I can find the water hidden in the trees and tell you which bugs to eat." He thumbed his nose. "And there is honey in the wood, but one must know where to find it."

"I'm Dyphestive." He looked about for the rest of his gear. His war mace was leaning against the wall by the doorway. He'd trusted Koll before, and he wasn't about to do it again. "Where are we? How long have I been out?"

Chopper rummaged through his cupboards and found a clay jug. "Ah, this will do it. This will help fix your friend." He hurried over to Grey Cloak with a slight limp in his step. "My hip is bad. It aches when it rains. Very little rain these days. He-he."

Dyphestive forced himself across the floor and grabbed Thunderash. "Touch him, and you will die!"

31

Before Dyphestive could lunge forward to cut Chopper off from Grey Cloak, someone—or some-thing—seized him by his hair. "Huh?" Dyphestive grunted in confusion.

All of a sudden, Dyphestive was being dragged outside with his arms flailing.

"Don't you touch Chopper," someone said in a deep, slow voice. "I'll hurt you."

"Not if I hurt you first." Dyphestive spun toward the unseen assailant and whacked him in the knee.

"Ow!" a giant of a man cried as he hopped up and down on his good leg. He was huge, bare chested, and had one eye in the middle of his bald head. He carried a lot of flab over his muscle, and he wore a loincloth. Many of his teeth were missing. He towered over Dyphestive by at least a foot. He reached for Dyphestive's war mace. "Give me that!"

Dyphestive went at the cyclops again and swung.

That time, the sun-bronzed brute caught the weapon in the ribs and trapped it at his side. He punched Dyphestive in the face with a ham-sized fist. Stars exploded behind Dyphestive's eyes. He shook it off and hit the cyclops in the ribs.

The cyclops winced and went down. "Ow! You hit hard for a little man!" He rose up to full height and balled his fists. "Grrrrrrrrr! I'm going to smash you to death!"

Chopper came rushing outside. "No! No! No! Tiny, stop! He's only protecting his friend!"

Tiny the cyclops glowered down at Dyphestive with his huge walnut-colored eye. "He tried to hurt you. I saw!"

Chopper approached with a hand out. "You were snooping, weren't you?"

"No," Tiny said with a guilty look.

"I told you about that. You get yourself into trouble when you snoop. Now, let go of the man's hammer," Chopper said.

"It's a mace," Dyphestive corrected.

Tiny snarled at Dyphestive, but he released the war hammer he'd trapped against his ribs. "I don't like you."

"Dyphestive, I realize that we are strangers, but on my word as a sand gnome, I will help your friend, and the sooner, the better," Chopper said.

Dyphestive slowly tore his gaze away from Tiny, who sat down on a log and began picking his nose. He cocked an eye at Chopper. "The last little fella said he'd help me too. He didn't, and he died for it."

Chopper caught his heavy look and swallowed. "Who might that have been?"

"A dwarf named Koll and the Scavengers."

The gnome's eyes grew to the size of saucers. "Y-you killed Koll? A brown-bearded dwarf?"

"Back at some fort. I killed him and the rest of the Scavenger men." Dyphestive waggled Thunderash at both of them. "If you're anything like them, I'll end you too."

"Please, friend, I promise you we're on your side. Koll and the Scavengers were nothing but a menace. None hated them more than we. They've taken from both of us, Tiny and I, hence we have an alliance."

"I don't believe him." Tiny stood up. He sniffed. "He stinks of lies."

"Do you really want to have another go at it?" Dyphestive warned. "I didn't hit you my hardest before."

"I didn't either!" Tiny shouted. "I'll rip your head off! Liar! You couldn't have killed all of them!"

"Go and see for yourself."

"No," Tiny said.

"We're very far from there, and we will keep it that way. If a warrior such as you says they are dead, then I'll believe it until I see otherwise." Chopper glanced at Tiny. "He doesn't take to many. Don't be offended. It's his nature not to trust."

"You said you could help my friend?"

"Yes. Yes. Come with me. I'm ready."

Dyphestive followed the gnome back inside the cottage and stooped down to keep his head from hitting the ceiling. Tiny stuck his big head in the doorway and sat down, blocking the exit. Dyphestive hadn't noticed it before, but Tiny had small spikelike horns on the top of his skull instead of hair.

Chopper picked up his clay jug and handed it to Dyphestive. "Smell that."

Dyphestive gave the gnome a wary look and took a faint sniff. "Vinegar?"

"Yes!" Chopper said elatedly. "Vinegar. The ticks and a few other creatures hate it." He took the jug from Dyphestive. "Watch this. It works like magic, but it isn't."

"I'm watching."

Chopper poured the vinegar on the desert blood tick, soaking it in the sour liquid. The insect didn't move. The gnome lifted a finger. "Be patient. It will take. Watch," he said in a hushed manner as he poured more vinegar on the gruesome bug with a bloody hump.

The desert tick quivered. Grey Cloak moaned.

"It's working, no worries," Chopper said.

The desert tick detached itself from Grey Cloak's back.

It turned like a crab, left then right, with its bloody hump wobbling.

Dyphestive could see the insect's beady bloodred eyes as it scurried down Grey Cloak's leg to the floor. It made its way across the room. He wanted to stomp its life out, but Tiny had other plans.

"Bloodberry!" Tiny scooped the tick up in his paw of a hand and popped the tick into his mouth. He bit down, and it squished all over. "Mmmmmmm."

Dyphestive's stomach turned inside out. He looked away from the cyclops. "That's nasty."

"Tiny isn't on a restricted diet. As long as it's not poisonous, he'll eat it, though he has eaten poison on occasion. It makes him very flatulent." Chopper winked at Dyphestive. "Don't be in the same room if that happens. It's bad enough as is."

Dyphestive caught a whiff of something foul and fanned his nose. "Yes, I'd say."

Tiny let out a rusty chuckle, took a deep breath, and said, "Smells good."

Looking over at Grey Cloak, Dyphestive asked Chopper, "What are you doing now?"

The gnome was busy rubbing the vinegar into the sore spot on Grey Cloak's back. The area was red, swollen, and pussy, but the web of veins covering his back was beginning to vanish.

"The vinegar will help with the healing. There's poison, but it's not fatal."

"When will he wake up?"

"The fact that he isn't dead is a miracle. I've never seen one go so long without dying." Chopper covered Grey Cloak with his cloak. "Interesting material, this garment. I will care for him, and hopefully he'll awake soon." He moved around the cot to Grey Cloak's head and looked into his eye. "Still glossy. That's good. He must be a strong elf."

Dyphestive nodded. "He is."

32

G rey Cloak remained in a coma. In the meantime, Dyphestive's time was occupied by Chopper and Tiny, who taught him the ways of the desert. It was midday, and the sun's heat felt like a furnace's.

"People die all the time out here and for no reason. The dirt offers plenty," Chopper said on more than one occasion. He said it again just then. "Now, look at this. It's a dead tree, long dead."

Dyphestive didn't know what sort of tree it was, but it wasn't very big, standing about ten feet tall. Most of its branches had fallen off long ago. "Yes, it's dead but good wood for burning."

"Well, that's obvious, but fire is no good if you have nothing to cook," Chopper replied.

"Stupid answer," Tiny added in his gruff voice.

"Show him, Tiny," Chopper said.

Tiny set his tremendous shoulders against the trunk of the tree and pushed. The dry timber cracked, and its root base heaved up. Grunting louder, Tiny put his legs into it and gave a bullish shove. The tree fell flat on the ground, busting several branches beneath it, which snapped loudly.

"Looky here, looky here," Chopper said as he gazed down into the hole the fallen tree had made. "An entire civilization."

Thousands of insects and their larvae lived in the hole.

"What a surprise, more bugs," Dyphestive said. They'd spent a lot of time searching out places with bugs in the ground. "You wouldn't be able to find any meat in the ground, would you?"

"Of course, of course," Chopper said as he stuffed a handful of crunchy bugs into his mouth. "We use the bugs for traps. Mmmm. Very delicious."

Dyphestive eyed Tiny. The cyclops had plenty of meat on his bones for a person who lived in the desert. His hairy belly bulged. "How does this one stay so fat eating bugs?"

"Not fat," the hulking brute said. "You fat, baby face."

Dyphestive arched a brow. "If you say so, donkey skull."

"I don't like you," Tiny said.

"Good to know." Dyphestive turned his back and walked away. He had nowhere to go so long as Grey Cloak was under. It didn't help that Streak had vanished. He'd told the dragon to go for help, and that was the last he'd seen him. He had other troubles on his mind. He had no idea when the time mural had put them. He knew they'd been transported to Sulter Slay, but it was unclear whether they were in the past or the future. "I think I'm going to head back to the cottage."

Tiny beat his chest with his fist. "No hunt. No eat!"

"You can have my share of the bugs." Dyphestive began the long walk back to the cottage with his head hung low. He'd learned enough about surviving the wild, barren stretches to find his way back safely. In a matter of two days, Chopper had filled him with enough knowledge to last him a lifetime. But after all that had happened, he felt empty and lost.

Back at Chopper's homestead, nothing had changed. A small barn, which was more of a shack, housed Tiny. Fencing surrounded the barn and the chicken pens inside, but it held no livestock.

The only livestock they could raise are lizards.

He kicked up dust as he passed a small, rickety wagon that, according to Chopper, Tiny had hauled him and Grey Cloak in. One of the slats in the wagon bed was gone, and there wasn't a bench seat to ride on either.

Thoughts of Crane and the others came to mind. A few days seemed like forever. For some reason, Chopper's bleak homestead made him think of the younger days in Havenstock working under Rhonna. He would love to see her warm, frowning face again. He missed her.

With a sigh, he headed over to the cottage. He wasn't one to complain about anything, the weather least of all, but the sun beat him down. He'd had enough and decided it was time to check on Grey Cloak. He stopped outside the curtain door.

Please be well. Please be well.

He entered the cottage and found Grey Cloak's cot empty. He picked up the cot and slung it aside. "No. No. No. No!"

He spun around the center of the small cottage, his eyes probing for answers, but he found none. Like a ghost, Grey Cloak was gone.

"Chopper!" Dyphestive shouted as he reached for his war mace lying in the back of the room. "Tiny! I knew this was a trick! I'm going to kill you!"

"Who are Chopper and Tiny?"

The voice was very familiar. Dyphestive spun on his heel just as Grey Cloak brushed the curtain door aside. "Grey?" he asked, his jaw hanging. Grey Cloak was dressed in his tattered gear and cloak. Full color had returned to his face. "Is it you?"

"Do you know any other elves who are this handsome?" Grey Cloak smirked. Patting his belly, he said, "I'm famished. I don't know where we are." His eyes scanned the room. "And the cupboards are as bare as a halfling's behind. Tell me you know where to find food."

Dyphestive charged across the room and swept his

blood brother up in his crushing arms. He jumped up and down. "I'm so glad you're back!"

"Easy!" Grey Cloak said. "My arm's still broken."

Dyphestive gently set him down, but he couldn't help but smile. "Sorry."

"All is well, brother." Grey Cloak messed up Dyphestive's hair. "So tell me, what in the flaming fence happened?"

33

Grey Cloak licked his greasy fingers. "This is the tastiest meat I've had in ages." He bit another hunk of seared flesh from the bone. "Marvelous. What sort of meat is this?"

It was early evening, and Chopper was huddled over a campfire, stirring up stew in a metal pot. Grinning from ear to ear, he said, "It's armadillo. Tasty. Now that's a compliment I like to hear." He eyed Tiny, who squatted near the fire, eating an armadillo's head. "This one never says anything kind."

"I like," Tiny commented as he crunched the armadillo skull in his jaws.

"Yes, such a glowing review." Chopper spooned some of his stew into a smaller bowl and handed it to Dyphestive. "Try this. It's seasoned. I have salt and ginger, you know."

Dyphestive had just finished eating a hunk of meat that was like chewing rawhide. He wasn't one to complain about food, but armadillo was awful. He dipped a wooden spoon into his bowl and sampled the stew. "Blech!" He spit it out.

"Too much salt?" Chopper asked.

"I'm not sure what you mean by salt." He swallowed down some water. "Or little."

"Oh, perhaps I overdid it. My salt is very, very strong." Chopper sat down on a large strip of driftwood and started eating.

Dyphestive gave Grey Cloak a suspicious look. "You like this?"

"I told you, I'm famished." Grey Cloak pointed with his leg bone. "Why didn't you tell me food could be so good? You used to eat it all the time."

Dyphestive scratched his head. "I thought you knew."

"I do now," Grey Cloak said cheerfully. "Chopper, more armadillo, please."

The small group finished every bit of the armadillo except its hide. Chopper had other uses for that.

As Grey Cloak licked each and every finger clean, he asked, "Now tell me again, what sort of creature incapacitated me?"

"A desert blood tick. Very dangerous if you don't know how to treat it," Chopper replied. "You had a good friend to look out for you. A blessing."

Grey Cloak nodded. "That I do." He stretched out his

arms and rolled them in wide circles as he glanced about. "Where are we?"

"Sulter Slay. Leagues away from Dwarf Skull. At least that's the closest place to here as of now," Chopper said.

"I see." Grey Cloak stood and scratched the side of his cheek. "And how did we get here?"

Dyphestive exchanged a worried glance with Chopper. He'd already told Grey Cloak what had happened twice. For some reason, nothing was sticking with the elf blood brother. He opened his mouth, but Grey Cloak cut him off.

"Oh, I remember." Grey Cloak pointed at Dyphestive. "You said we came through a tunnel."

"No, a time mural," he corrected.

"Ah, yes, a time mural, and it was in a wizard tower." Grey Cloak began to pace around the campfire. When he spoke, he spoke inquisitively. "We were fighting a dragon and fled through the tunnel?"

"No, it wasn't a dragon. It was a wizard, and it wasn't a tunnel, it was an archway," Dyphestive argued. "Do you remember anything? Tatiana, Gossamer, the underlings?"

"Do the underlings taste like chicken?"

Dyphestive slapped his forehead.

"What is underling? Tiny want to eat underling," Tiny said.

Dyphestive got up from his seat, walked over to Grey Cloak, and grabbed him by the cloak. He looked him dead in the eye and said, "Tell me you're fooling with me." He shook him. "Can't you remember anything?"

Grey Cloak smirked. "I'm trying."

Dyphestive's shoulders sank, and he let go of his friend. In a soft voice, he said, "You remember me, don't you?"

"Of course I do. You are Festive, my oldest and dearest friend. We've hardly ever been apart." He motioned in circles with his hands. "It's all of these other issues I'm fuzzy about. You mention names. I see faces, but that is all." He patted Dyphestive on the shoulder. "It could be worse, I suppose. It's a beautiful night. I think I'll take a stroll. Don't wait up."

With a heavy heart, Dyphestive joined Chopper by the fire as he watched Grey Cloak wander into the night.

"You seem gravely concerned," Chopper said.

"His gray matter is rattled."

"Elf is dumb like armadillo," Tiny commented with a chuckle.

"Your friend was on the threshold of death. He's still healing. Give him time to come out of it." Chopper glanced over his shoulder. "Perhaps it's a new world to him."

"Well, I had that happen to me before. Bad things happened because of it," he said.

"What sort of bad things?" Chopper asked.

"I killed a few people," Dyphestive said with a deep frown. Even though he was known as Iron Bones and under Drysis's influence, he could still see the images of the halfling men he'd slaughtered. It woke him from sleep sometimes. It was impossible to erase the memory from his mind.

"It sounds like you've killed many. That will change a man as the bodies stack up. Do you fear that your friend will become a reckless killer?"

"No, I fear that I'll lose the best friend I've ever had."

Chopper nodded. "Be patient." He slurped more of his stew. "And eat. It's good for your spirits."

Tiny let out a rumbling fart. "That will keep the spirits away. Hah!"

"Shew!" Dyphestive stood and walked away. "I'll be in the cottage. Keep an eye on Grey Cloak, will you?"

"No worries. He has nowhere to go," Chopper said with a smile. "Perhaps a long walk in the cool air will do him much good. One day at a time, my friend. One day at a time."

"I hope." Inside the cottage, Dyphestive found the cot he'd been using and overfilled it with his big body. "What am I going to do with Grey Cloak and his addled mind? I need him."

Worst of all was that Grey Cloak hadn't even asked about Streak. The elf and the dragon were bonded. Grey Cloak should've at least mentioned him.

Dyphestive lay his head on a dingy cushion and repeated what Chopper had said. "One day at a time. One day at a time." He dozed off.

Chopper woke him later, shaking him hard. "Wake, my friend, wake!"

He sat up. "What is it?"

Chopper gripped a floppy-brimmed hat in his tiny mitts. "It's your friend. I fear we lost him."

34

"Apologies! Apologies!" Chopper pleaded.

Through stiff winds, Dyphestive was carrying the sand gnome in his arms like a loaf of bread. "I don't want to hear it. If you set me up, I'm going to pulverize your bones."

Chopper frantically waved his arms. "We're friends. I swear it. I wouldn't trifle with a slayer such as you. Your friend is fast, very fast like a jackrabbit."

All Dyphestive could do was grind his teeth. He never should have let Grey Cloak out of sight in his condition, but he'd never imagined Grey Cloak would run off without having an idea of where he was going. It was madness.

"Where is Tiny? Is he close?"

"Almost there. He waits." Chopper pointed toward a

rocky hillside bathed in moonlight. "Not far at all. I think I see him."

They caught up with Tiny, who stood like a statue on the hard terrain. He wore a large pack between his wide shoulders. He snorted lungfuls of air through his wide nostrils and cast his heavy stare on Dyphestive. "Put down Chopper."

"I don't take orders from you, One Eye. Say please."

"Say what?" Tiny replied.

"Never mind." He set Chopper down but held him by the collar. "Where's my brother?"

"Elf is not your brother. You man, he elf. You speak dumbly," Tiny added.

Dyphestive lifted his war mace. "You're dumbly!"

"Do you still have the scent, Tiny?" Chopper asked quickly.

"Tiny smell the elf. The elf in the Burnt Hills. He not come out. I would know." Tiny spit on the ground and glared at Dyphestive. "Only death in those hills."

"Then why didn't you stop him?" Dyphestive asked.

"Maybe he don't like you," Tiny suggested.

"I'm going to bust your skull."

Tiny leaned forward, showing the small, hard horns on the top of his head. "You try first. I go second."

Dyphestive looked away. "I though you said you lost him."

"We lost him in the Burnt Hills, a terrible place," Chopper said.

"Why is it so terrible?"

"It's haunted."

"What do you mean, haunted? Ghosts? Spirits? Devils? What's in there?"

"I can't say. No one I've ever known who has gone in has come out."

Dyphestive picked up Chopper by the collar. "Today's your lucky day. We're going to go find out what happened to them."

"No, no, please, no!" Chopper begged. His little legs ran through the air. "It's not wise to go in there."

"You should have thought that through before you lost my friend."

Tiny grabbed Dyphestive's shoulder. "Let him go!"

Dyphestive walloped Tiny in the gut with the butt end of Thunderash. Tiny doubled over. "If you're so worried about your little friend, you can come along, too, stinky. But keep your filthy paws to yourself." He marched straight for the Burnt Hills.

"Listen to me. Listen to me, Dyphestive, please," Chopper said in a desperate voice. "I'm a survivor, not an adventurer. I'm not equipped to fight. Look at me. I don't even have a weapon of any sort. If you take me in there, I will certainly die." His little body trembled. "I restored your friend's life. Please, restore me."

Dyphestive stopped and sighed. The last thing he needed to do was drag a gnome who was squealing like a pig into the heart of an unknown enemy's territory. He let Chopper down. "Go. I'll settle this alone."

"I'm sorry, friend, but I live in the burning wild not because I'm brave but because I'm a coward. All I can do is wish you well."

Dyphestive looked down on Chopper's little frame. "I have a feeling I'll need a lot more help than that." He took a knee, picked up a handful of dirt, and rubbed it into his hands. "Thanks for the help, Chopper. But if I find out you betrayed me, I'll—"

"I know, pulverize my bones."

Dyphestive marched over the black and dusty plains toward the Burnt Hills. The wind picked up as he closed in on the stark hill climb. The scent of brimstone lingered in the air, and the rocky spires ahead began to howl.

Even in the darkness, Dyphestive could make out an old path. He hoped to catch a glimpse of Grey Cloak's footfalls, but gusty night winds took any evidence of that away. At the base of the rocky hills, he began his climb into the dark fortress of nature.

Grey Cloak, what are you thinking?

He'd just gotten his friend back only to lose him again. That wasn't the only friend he'd lost. He'd left behind Tatiana, Zora, Razor, Anya, Bowbreaker, and Leena, too, as well as many others—Crane and Jakoby, not to mention

Tanlin, Lythlenion, and Rhonna. He hoped in his heart they'd survived. He hoped, somehow, someway, the threat of Black Frost was gone.

An eerie chill fell over him then went through his skin and into his bones. The wind that whistled through the rocks sounded like living things letting out their last gasps of life. Something was alive in those hills. The scent of death lingered.

Come on, Grey Cloak. Where are you?

35

The Burnt Hills were an unending catacomb of rocks made up of jagged boulders, gulches, and deep gullies. With his ears peeled and his eyes wide open, Dyphestive traversed the rugged terrain as quietly as he could. He peered into every nook and crested every crag but saw no sign of Grey Cloak, or anything else living for that matter.

His strong fingers found purchase on a rock shelf, and he hauled himself up to one of the higher peaks. His broad body wasn't meant for climbing the narrow ledges, but the strength in his nimble fingertips saved him from falling time and again.

He was more of a mountain goat, surefooted and slow, but could do nothing the likes of what he'd seen Grey Cloak do. Grey Cloak crawled walls like a spider.

At the top of the peak, he stopped and took a breath. He could see the surrounding plains—leagues of nothing that appeared like a black sea. The wind rustled his hair, and his heart beat in his ears. He felt totally alone.

Grey, why would you even come here? Better yet, did you even come here, or am I a lamb being delivered to the slaughter?

Dyphestive had put his faith in a gnome he didn't know. All he could do was judge Chopper by his actions. But the entire series of events had been bizarre. Grey Cloak wasn't himself when he left, but he was alive when he very well could have been dead. Dyphestive was thankful for that much at least.

The howling winds picked up and whistled like a banshee's hollow screams.

A chill raced down Dyphestive's spine as he felt feathery fingers on his neck. He twisted around. Something was there, or something was in the air. *I felt that.*

The eerie howling sounded like a call from beyond, beckoning Dyphestive to venture deeper into the black hills. He resumed his journey into the very heart of the hillside, spiraling downward into the depths hidden from the moonlight.

His eyes adjusted, and he traversed a passage zigzagging through the rocks that was calling out to him. The droning wind sounded like the voices of the dead calling, *Come. Come. Come.*

He went, step after step, deeper into the blackness. He

jumped over a narrow chasm with glimmering eyes shining in its depths. He looked again. The bright eyes were gone.

The catacombs ended in front of a cave mouth big enough to swallow a middling dragon.

Come. Come. Come.

Columns were carved out of the rock face, fashioning it like an ancient long-abandoned temple. Yet something lived. He heard it.

Come. Come. Come.

The words were faint and the speech unfamiliar, but he had no doubt about the meaning.

Come. Come. Come.

Dyphestive broke out in a cold sweat as icy fingers tickled his neck again. He spun around.

Grey Cloak stood ten paces behind him. The wind rustled his cloak. His hood covered his head, and his sword and dagger hung in his hands.

Dyphestive couldn't see his brother's eyes. "Grey?" There was no mistaking the height and build, but the stooped stance threw him off. "Is that you?"

The howling winds died down. Silence fell over the black hills.

Grey Cloak took a few slow steps forward. He spun his sword in a circle at his side.

Dyphestive lifted up his war mace and swallowed. "Grey, it's me, Dyphestive. What's wrong?"

The elf came two steps closer. He spun his sword again.

"Grey, what are you doing?"

"I am not he," Grey Cloak responded in a strange, cold voice. "I am me." He pulled back his hood with his dagger hand. His eyes were wide open and pure white. "Who are you, invader?"

"Grey, it's me, Dyphestive." He stepped back toward the cave, his neck hairs standing on end. "Stop fooling around. You need to come with me."

"This is sacred ground," Grey Cloak said. "You—oh man—are an invader." The possessed elf jumped forward.

Dyphestive hopped back, deeper into the cave.

A scuffle of claws over dirt caught his ears. Something charged out of the darkness with its jaws open wide.

Dyphestive swung into the jaws of death. Thunderash crashed into the monster's jaw. A thunderclap followed.

Krak-boooooom!

The monster was a giant eight-legged lizard, and its momentum carried it crashing into Dyphestive, where it came to a stop and died, its tongue hanging out of its mouth.

"Nooo!" Grey Cloak called out in a haunted voice. "You slew my servant." His bright eyes locked on Dyphestive. Grey Cloak came at him with his sword. "You will die!"

Dyphestive's legs were pinned underneath the lizard's massive skull. He pushed out from underneath it and lifted his war mace in time to block Grey Cloak's strike. He swiped at Grey Cloak's feet with his arm.

The elf skipped away. "Invader, you will die!" Grey Cloak came at him again with his blades jabbing.

Dyphestive popped up to his feet. Using the length of his war mace, he kept the attacking elf at bay. "I don't know who you are, but get out of my friend's body."

"This is my body!" Grey Cloak slipped by the war mace and slashed Dyphestive across the shoulder. "Your blood is mine. Everything in Ruunalin is mine! Prepare to die!"

36

It took everything Dyphestive had to keep up with the speed of Grey Cloak's striking blades. He used both ends of his war mace to block the fast strikes. If not for his training with the Doom Riders, he would have been cut to ribbons as they danced in the darkness.

It's times like this when I wish I had some armor. How do I stop him without hurting him?

Whoever had control of Grey Cloak's body wasn't perfect. The sword strikes were fast but wild. It had full control of the elf's fluid frame, but it didn't have the skill, which bought Dyphestive time.

I need to knock him out without hurting him.

It was easier said than done. Grey Cloak hopped out of harm's way as quickly as a jackrabbit whenever Dyphestive reached for him.

I need to get him to the ground.

Grey Cloak was strong, but he wasn't a match for Dyphestive. He only needed to figure out a way to grab Grey Cloak before he could slice his fingers off.

Wait for it. Wait for it.

A sword strike whistled by his ear. A dagger punched at his gut. Dyphestive blocked the next sword strike and kicked at him.

Grey Cloak jumped away like a springing deer. "You will die, invader. Ruunalin is mine!"

Dyphestive changed tactics. "Who are you?"

"I am Elkhorn Blackstone, master of stone."

"Are you a dwarf?" he asked.

"I am the lord of the rock and reaver of invaders." Grey Cloak charged, his weapons flashing. "They all die. You shall die next!"

Dyphestive jabbed his war mace out like a spear and caught Grey Cloak in the shoulder. The hard blow knocked the possessed elf backward. Without hesitation, Dyphestive pounced on his blood brother. He landed on top of Grey Cloak but not before Grey Cloak's dagger stabbed him in the thigh. He dropped his war mace and went after Grey Cloak's wrists.

Grey Cloak squirmed away, but Dyphestive filled his hands with cloak and yanked his blood brother down. They grappled over the hard ground, rolling over one another.

Dyphestive pinned Grey Cloak down by the wrists and wrenched the blades free. "Stop struggling. Grey Cloak, I know you're in there. Listen to me. It's your friend, Dyphestive."

Grey Cloak kicked him in the groin.

Dyphestive grimaced and held fast. "Don't do that again, Elkhorn Blackstone."

"You cannot defeat me! I live forever!" Grey Cloak thrashed about with supernatural strength, pushing Dyphestive back. "I am stronger!" he said with glowing white-hot eyes.

A heavy net dropped from the sky and fell on them.

"Remove these bonds! Remove them at once, invaders!" Grey Cloak shouted.

From the darkness, Chopper approached with a hunk of rock glowing in his fist. The green hue of the stone illuminated his eyes.

"What treachery is this?" Dyphestive demanded.

Tiny's hulking frame moved into view. He had a pouch in his hand.

"Do it now," Chopper ordered.

The cyclops removed sparkling sand from the pouch. He sprinkled it over himself and Chopper. He moved closer to Dyphestive and Grey Cloak and flung the dust over both of them.

"You will pay dearly for that!" Grey Cloak screamed. "I'll take your life, one eye!"

Dyphestive spit the dust from his mouth. "What did you do, traitors?"

Chopper locked his eyes on Grey Cloak and began to chant. The green rock in his hand beat and pulsated. The wind picked up, stirring the dusty ground. The longer he chanted, the stronger and louder his words became.

Grey Cloak cringed and cowered. "Nooo! Nooo!" He shielded his face with his hands, and his voice became evil and deeper. "I will slaughter you, invader! I'll destroy you! Your family! Your homes will rot, and your bones will be fed to the hounds of death! Go away!"

The fierce winds blasted through Chopper's beard and clothing, but he stood as firm as a stone. "Return to the grave, Elkhorn Blackstone! The grave awaits!"

Grey Cloak let out a howl as a ghostly apparition pulled free from his body. It hovered and hissed like a snake. Setting its burning eyes on Dyphestive, it dove at him and bounced off.

"Noooo!" it cried.

The spirit flew at Tiny and bounced away from the sparkling sand on his body. It tried to enter twice more, turned on Chopper, and let out an earsplitting shriek.

Dyphestive covered his ears as he watched the spirit convulse, spasm, and explode into ghostly ashes.

The wind died down. The stone in Chopper's hand cooled. Sweat glistened on his grimy face as he staggered forward, stumbled, and fell. Rolling onto his back, Chopper said, "Well done. We did it."

BACK AT CHOPPER'S COTTAGE, Grey Cloak was as cheerful and bright-eyed as ever. He sipped on tea made with honey as he counted the gold coins in the palm of his hand. "It's a notable score."

"Agreed," Chopper said as he refilled Dyphestive's earthenware mug. "Dwarven tombs are often lavish. We're all very fortunate to have survived that ordeal. The shade of Elkhorn Blackstone was a powerful one. Over the years, I'd only suspected what we were dealing with, but if not for you, Dyphestive, being so brave, we never would have rid ourselves of the menace."

Dyphestive nodded as he sipped his elixir. "I'm glad I have my friend back. That's all that matters."

Chopper toasted them with his mug. "We're blessed. The shade of Elkhorn called out to the elf and caught his ear when he was feebleminded. I apologize that we lost him, but it turned out for the better. The Burnt Hills are free of death, and that treasure will serve us well. We'll be able to supply ourselves for years."

"You can say that again," Grey Cloak said as he filled his inner pockets with gold. He plucked one item free of his cloak, a ruby dragon charm. "Not to mention, we have this. It should come in handy."

"A prize indeed," Chopper said as he teetered through the room.

Grey Cloak caught Dyphestive looking at him. "What?"

"How's your arm?" he asked.

When Grey Cloak had battled him, his brother's arm hadn't given him any trouble at all. It had appeared fully healed.

Grey Cloak rolled his shoulder and rubbed his arm. "It's as good as the other one. You'll have to forgive me, brother. I'm hazy on some details, but my mind clears for the better by the moment." He placed his hand on Dyphestive's shoulder and winked. "I'm back to normal but possibly illuminated."

"What do you mean?"

"It's hard to explain, but I found myself inside my body and out of it. I've been drained by a tick and possessed by a dwarf." He dropped the dragon charm inside his inner pocket. "It changes an elf. Imagine if you had Rhonna living in your head. It was similar to that but much worse."

Dyphestive shrugged.

Grey Cloak eyed the ugly wounds on his brother's arms and legs. "I'm sorry about that. I don't remember anything that happened before the gnome ripped the dwarf spirit from my body."

"It's fine. Chopper stitched me up well." He raised a brow. "What are we going to do now?"

"I suggest you travel to Dwarf Skull. You will need supplies if you're going to journey north again. It takes lots of water."

Dyphestive nodded and headed outside, where the morning sun shone in his eyes.

Tiny had rolled up his net and was stuffing it back into its sack. The cyclops glanced away from Dyphestive as he approached.

That didn't stop Dyphestive from offering his hand. "Thanks for helping out."

Tiny grunted, but he took Dyphestive's hand anyway and tried to break his bones. "Tiny stronger, human."

Dyphestive squeezed back and watched Tiny's eyes widen. "Are you sure about that?"

The cyclops tore his grip away. "Tiny sure. Now go away."

37

Chopper and Tiny escorted Grey Cloak and Dyphestive to Dwarf Skull, and it wasn't anything like they'd expected. The brothers stood side by side with their mouths open.

"That's Dwarf Skull?" Grey Cloak asked. He studied the league-long fortified structure built around natural rocks and spectacular pinnacles.

"That's it," Chopper said proudly, as if it were his own. "There's nothing like it in the world, they say, but I don't know. I haven't been anywhere else."

Dwarf Skull sat on a plateau, like Raven Cliff, but was mountainous in size. The structure rested on a sheet of dark stone. It was a solid wall of black rock forty feet high with battle towers spaced evenly all around it. A great pinnacle stood in the middle of the monstrous structure, overlooking everything for leagues. Brilliant flags billowed at the top of the battlements, and dwarven soldiers marched along the top wall with spears and halberds.

"It's as big as Monarch City," Dyphestive commented.

"Er... will they let us in there?" Grey Cloak asked. It might as well have been Black Frost's temple, as ominous and foreboding as it appeared.

"Sure, sure, all are welcome if they pay a tribute." Chopper patted the purse on his hip. "You have more than enough to cover that."

"You're going in with us, aren't you?" Dyphestive asked the gnome.

Chopper rubbed his chin. "Er... as much as we enjoy your company, Tiny and I prefer to move on and conduct our business elsewhere. You've helped us. We've helped you." He thumbed his nose and winked. "And don't mention Elkhorn Blackstone. The less they know, the better. Best to you in Dwarf Skull."

The brothers watched the cyclops and gnome wander toward the distant farms and villages of the bleak surroundings.

"Shall we finish the journey to Dwarf Skull?" Grey Cloak asked. "I'm dying to see what's behind those walls, and I'm famished."

"You're really hungry?" Dyphestive asked.

"I have a newfound appreciation for the finer things in life. It's important that I enjoy them when I can." Grey

Cloak glanced up. He'd hoped that Streak would appear, but he hadn't. "Perhaps it's for the better."

"Perhaps what's for the better?" Dyphestive asked.

"Streak is probably safer. I'm glad you sent him for help, but I am worried about him."

"Me too. I'm sorry, but I didn't know what else to do," Dyphestive said.

"Cheer up, brother. You saved me. I couldn't be more thankful. Streak will show eventually." Grey Cloak led the march to Dwarf Skull's entrance leagues away. On their way, they passed villages made up of stone huts and fields of dry farmland. They saw many hardened and dirty grim-faced dwarves who didn't blink or wave. Even the children didn't play.

"Brother, I have a feeling something isn't quite right about this place."

"So do I," Dyphestive said as he surveyed his surroundings. "If you ask me, this place is in short supply of everything."

"There's only one way to know for sure. Beyond those walls, we'll find answers." Grey Cloak picked up the pace and didn't stop until they were at the base of Dwarf Skull's league-long plateau. The cliffs were sheer and hundreds of feet high. Bird nests were scattered along the ledges. Flocks of little birds flew in and out. "I don't see an entrance. Odd."

"I don't either." Dyphestive scratched his head. "Maybe we shouldn't assume the entrance is in the north. Perhaps it's in the south or the east or the west. I'm surprised Chopper didn't mention it."

"I'd say that's why this place is well fortified. It's a mountain, or a sawed-off one at least." Grey Cloak picked up the pace to a trot with Dyphestive huffing along behind him. They jogged over a mile before they spotted a cave opening at the base of the mountain guarded by heavily armored dwarves.

The dwarves were in full battle array, with suits made from plates of blackened iron and full helmets complete with nose guards. Each and every one of them was as stout as a chimney, and they stood perfectly still with a spear or halberd—fitting their size—in hand.

Grey Cloak approached with caution as he eyed the cave backdrop behind the dwarven ranks. A closed iron portcullis blocked the mouth of the cave. He saw nothing but the deeper bowels of the cave on the other side. None in the dwarven ranks moved a muscle as he walked by them as if they were stones.

At the portcullis were several soldiers, and Grey Cloak asked, "May we enter?"

The dwarves didn't bat an eye. They looked straight forward without so much as a nod.

He exchanged a puzzled look with his brother, shrugged, and tapped a dwarf on the shoulder. "Pardon—"

The dwarves moved like a single unit and exploded into

action. They surrounded Grey Cloak and Dyphestive with halberds and spears pointed at their chests.

Standing back-to-back, Grey Cloak and Dyphestive lifted their hands in surrender.

Grey Cloak finished his sentence. "—me?"

38

DWARF SKULL

"You weren't supposed to touch them. Why did you touch them?" Dyphestive asked.

"It was a friendly tap. I didn't think it would be misconstrued as an attack," Grey Cloak said as he watched the dwarves wind chain around him and Dyphestive. "You could have run."

Dyphestive eyed the portcullis. "I have a feeling that if I did, they would've poured out of that mountain like bearded ants."

Grey Cloak made another plea from where he sat on the ground. "We came to buy water and food for our journey. We'll pay to enter. We meant no harm." The dwarves' eyes were as hard as coal, and they didn't so much as grunt. "And I thought Rhonna was sour. Do you know if she ever had children?"

"Don't provoke them," Dyphestive warned.

"I think we passed that point."

The dwarves tightened the chains, but one of them vanished in a cleft near the portcullis. Grey Cloak saw the dwarf go. *Ah, a secret entrance. That should come in handy.* The dwarves dropped sacks over their heads. *Or not.*

"I think I fared better when you traveled with a blood tick," Dyphestive said in a muted voice.

"Ha ha. Don't worry. You know I'll get us out of this. I always do." The grinding of greased gears and rattling metal pricked his ears. The portcullis was going up. *Ah, that's where the dwarf went, to let us in.* "See, brother? I have it under control. All part of the plan."

Assisted by the dwarves, they were marched inside the cave. Grey Cloak could hear their bootsteps echoing inside the chamber, and the light dimmed. The air cooled as well, and they moved upward to a higher elevation.

"I love surprises, don't you, brother?" Grey Cloak asked.

"Not as much as you, apparently."

On the trip to Dwarf Skull, they'd discussed using discretion with their names. They had no idea who might be looking for them or at what point in time they had arrived. Of course, Grey Cloak doubted any of that was true at all. It seemed far-fetched that the time mural would move them forward or backward in time. It was inconceivable, yet they'd been teleported from one place to another somehow.

Back in the Wizard Watch, Gossamer had explained how the wizards could move from one tower to another and how the time mural was out of control, but Grey Cloak had never seen it work firsthand until they'd wound up in Sulter Slay.

"It's getting stuffy inside this hood," he commented. "You wouldn't happen to have anything more breathable, like cotton perhaps?"

One of the dwarven soldiers shoved him in the back. He intentionally faltered and landed on a knee. "Easy, it's hard enough to walk when you can't see, let alone be shoved." It wasn't true, of course. Grey Cloak was trying to gauge his captors and location.

They'd climbed steadily up over five hundred steps so far. Even though he couldn't see, he counted eight different sets of dwarven boots marching them deeper into the plateau.

Now might be a good time to turn back and get out of here. The deeper we go, the harder it will be to leave.

He cleared his throat as the strong-armed dwarves lifted him back to his feet.

"See it through," Dyphestive muttered.

That was all the confirmation Grey Cloak needed. If Dyphestive had wanted to turn back, he would have made a comment otherwise.

No turning back now.

They marched another hour through a labyrinth of

corridors before they came to a stop in a room flooded in torchlight.

A fireplace crackled, and Grey Cloak could feel the fire's warmth on his fingers. The dwarves undid their chains, and he could hear them clink as they were carried out of the room. All eight pairs of dwarven boots left. A door shut, and they were sealed inside a chamber.

Grey Cloak lifted the sack from his face. He exchanged a look with Dyphestive, who was removing his hood as well. At the same time, they turned to look at the source of the fire.

A stone fireplace as tall as a man burned in the center of the room. A chimney made by dwarven stonework kissed the ceiling of the chamber and vanished. Two dwarven soldiers were posted on each side of the fireplace. They wore full plate armor, and black helms covered their heads. Braided chestnut beards spilled out from underneath. Each of them carried a war hammer, and like the stone, they did not move.

Another figure stood in front of the fireplace with its back to the brothers and its rough hands locked behind its back. The figure's hair had many braids in the back and a bun on top. Most of the hair was gray with shades of brown. The figure wore a dwarven tunic that covered it to its toes.

The brothers exchanged another glance.

Grey Cloak shrugged and cleared his throat. "Nice fire."

The figure answered, "What have you two bent horse-shoes done?" The figured turned and faced them.

Grey Cloak's eyes widened.

Dyphestive blurted out, "Rhonna!"

39

Dyphestive didn't make it within ten steps of Rhonna before the two soldiers swooped in and blocked his path. He stopped in his tracks and looked over them to Rhonna. "I was only going to give her a hug."

"By the hammer of the forges, you're bigger than an ox. Stand down," Rhonna said in her rugged voice. "He's a friend."

The soldiers parted, and she moved between them.

Dyphestive took a knee and hugged her. "I never thought I'd be so happy to see anyone."

"I know how you feel." She patted him on the back. "I might be tough as a nut, but you're about to crack me."

Dyphestive let go. "Sorry."

"No worries. I need my bones cracked."

Grey Cloak slipped beside her. He noticed the hard lines on her face had deepened. "I never thought there would be a day when I'd be so happy to see you, Rhonna." He eyed her hair. "Where'd all the gray come from? Did you see a ghost?"

"I wish I had." Rhonna gave Grey Cloak her usual stern look. "Where have you two been?"

"The question is, what are you doing here?" he asked.

"Respect your elder and the one who bailed you out from my kin."

"You first?"

Rhonna's jaw clenched.

Dyphestive stepped in. "Let's not go back to our old ways. Rhonna, we were in the Wizard Watch, east of the Great River of Arrowwood."

"You don't have to tell her anything, Dyphestive," Grey Cloak said. "It appears she's changed."

"It's Rhonna. She hasn't changed." Dyphestive looked about the chamber. "If I can't trust her, no one can be trusted."

"Huh," Rhonna said. She moved away from the fire to a bar with wooden barrels on it. She grabbed a tankard from underneath and opened a barrel tap. A dark walnut ale poured out. "Changed doesn't begin to describe it. And yes, I have changed. I've changed because I'm no longer Rhonna, a blacksmith from Havenstock, but rather Rhonna the Monarch Queen of Dwarf Skull."

"Ah, delusions of grandeur. How convenient." Grey Cloak crossed his arms. "And how did this come about?"

Rhonna drained her tankard and refilled it. "Would either one of you donkey skulls like a drink?"

"Make it two," Grey Cloak said.

The blood brothers sat down at a stone table with benches on either side.

Rhonna sat across from them and shoved a tankard to each. "Drink, maybe that will loosen your tongue."

Grey Cloak took a sip, and his face puckered. "No wonder you're so bitter. Is this what you've been drinking all your life?"

Dyphestive guzzled it down. "I like it."

Grey Cloak took another drink. "I guess it's like you, Rhonna, an acquired taste. Now you were saying about how you came to be the Monarch Queen of Dwarf Skull?"

Rhonna eyed him. "I have to admit, I'm glad *you* haven't changed. You've both grown, but you haven't changed." She drank deeply. "It's as refreshing as dwarven ale after hours on the battlefield."

"We went through a time mural in the Wizard Watch," Dyphestive said to her. "That's how we wound up here."

"Why don't you tell her everything?" Grey Cloak asked sarcastically.

"I will." Dyphestive filled Rhonna in on their last adventure at the Wizard Watch. He explained how they'd come across the dragon-charm helm and used the Figurine of Heroes to summon the underlings, Catten and Verbard.

Rhonna rose from her bench and shook her head. Under her breath, she said, "I knew. I knew in the depths of my belly that you had something to do with it." She eyed Grey Cloak. "You gamble. You take the short path. Do you know what you've done?"

Grey Cloak shrank under her gaze. "I have a feeling that I better have another drink." He drank half the tankard. "Go on."

The wrinkles in the corners of Rhonna's tired eyes deepened. She sat back down. "Do you know how long it's been since I last saw you?"

"Why do I have the feeling that I don't want to know the answer to that?" he asked.

Dyphestive leaned forward. "How long?"

"Twenty seasons."

Grey Cloak spit up his drink. "Twenty seasons? You jest!"

"I wish it were a jest. Believe me, I'd be back in Havenstock, hammering away at the forge, but instead I'm here."

Dyphestive swallowed. He reached over and covered Rhonna's fist in his palm. "You really mean this? It's been twenty seasons since you saw us last." There were two seasons in every year, hence ten years had passed. "I can't believe that."

"Believe it. It's the year sixty twenty-three. Gapoli is

under the full control of Black Frost and those underlings." She glared at Grey Cloak. "Whatever you brought here accelerated Black Frost's plans. He's more ruthless now than ever, and with those underlings as his henchmen, he's unstoppable."

Grey Cloak tilted his chair on its back two legs. "So, does this make me twenty-seven years old, or am I still seventeen?" He needled his chin. "Wait, I'm eighteen, or am I twenty-eight?"

Rhonna looked at him. "Do you find this a laughing matter? Do you know how many thousands have died over the past ten years because of your error?"

"Ho, Rhonna, you can't pin the blame on Grey Cloak. He only did what he thought best," Dyphestive said. He shook his tankard from side to side. "Can I get another? I have a feeling I'm going to need it."

40

The list went on as Rhonna told the story of the demise of Gapoli. After the underlings had arrived, the world had fallen under a landslide of evil.

Grey Cloak hung on her words, but he feigned distraction even as fear grew in the pit of his stomach. He paced around the table, juggling plates and saucer cups. *It can't all be my fault.*

"I knew that Black Frost was at war with the Dragon Riders and thought, as long as they were defending the skies, he would leave the rest of the world alone—Black Frost would only want a tribute." Rhonna shook her head. "At least that was how the Monarchs saw it in Dwarf Skull, but that wasn't the case.

"Black Frost built up his armies. The Black Guard invaded the smaller towns first and started recruiting more soldiers into their armies. Before we knew it, it was a black wave. They took over Portham and invaded Havenstock. I saw the handwriting on the wall before it happened. I fled."

"How long ago was this?" Dyphestive asked.

"Five years or so," she said as she wiped her mouth. "I came home to find refuge, but instead, I discovered that generations of my family had been slaughtered, generations of Monarchs." Her hard voice softened. "I never told you this, but I'm a Monarch legacy—the great-granddaughter of Ironthumb Warboot. He was the Monarch king of Dwarf Skull. My brothers and sisters were killed in a surprise Risker invasion.

"When I arrived, I was first in line to the throne. Black Frost still has forces here, but he lets me lead so long as I don't cause trouble. Not to mention, he controls the Twin Rivers, which allow our valley to thrive. He dammed them at the Iron Hills. Water flows but only because he lets it. If he wants, he can turn Dwarf Skull into a wasteland."

"This is madness," Dyphestive said. He stood up and punched his fist into his hand. "How can this be? Isn't there anyone in this world who can stand up to him? Him and those underlings?"

Rhonna sighed. "I have to admit that I never imagined anything like this. I thought the Sky Riders would take him down, but when I found out that he killed them, well, my heart turned to wax." She shook her head. "And those underlings. I saw them with my own eyes. I've never seen such evil. I'd hate to imagine a world full of them. They destroy everything."

Grey Cloak cringed. He'd gotten more than an eyeful of the underlings the first go-round. "I can't believe they're still here. They should have vanished into the figurine, but they flicked it through the time mural and stopped themselves from being transported back. It could be in any time or place."

"As much as I didn't care for the elf, Tatiana, she was right. You gambled one too many times," Rhonna said as she refilled her tankard. "It came back and bit us. It came back and bit us all. I don't fault you for it. No one could have seen this coming. I'm glad you're both here and I found you first."

"What do you mean?" Grey Cloak asked.

"They're still looking for you. You, Dyphestive, the figurine, Sky Riders, any enemy that they think can stop them. That's why I'm glad I found you first. When you used my name, word got back to me of your descriptions. I didn't think it could be, but it was. I'm glad."

"Are you telling me that after we've been gone ten years, Black Frost is still looking for us?" Dyphestive asked.

"Most likely. After all, the two of you continue to slip through his claws," she said.

"What about the others?" he asked.

"Others, who?" Rhonna asked.

"Tatiana, Zora, Bowbreaker, Lythlenion," Grey Cloak said, "have you seen any of them?"

Rhonna sadly shook her head. "I've only heard rumors."

Grey Cloak stopped juggling and set down the objects. "What rumors?"

"Every member of Talon is either imprisoned or dead. Worst of all, Bowbreaker has been captured by the elven Monarch queen of Arrowwood, Esmarelda. She aligned herself with Black Frost early on."

"What about Anya? Has there been any sign of her?"

"She was the last Sky Rider. The Riskers were proud to announce during one of their routine visits that they slew her."

"Which Riskers?" Dyphestive asked.

Rhonna sneered. "Two young blondes lead them, older than you. They call themselves—"

"Dirklen and Magnolia," Grey Cloak said. "Are those two windbags leading the Riskers? It figures."

"They'd be thirty years old now," Dyphestive said.

"You know them?" Rhonna asked.

"Oh, we know them. That's how we came to Haven-stock, to get away from the likes of them and Black Frost." Grey Cloak couldn't believe his pointed ears. Everything in the world that could go wrong had gone wrong and all in a matter of days in his time. "I'm going to fix this."

"How?" Rhonna asked.

"I don't know how, but I'm going to try. I broke it. I'll fix it."

"No, brother," Dyphestive said, "we'll fix this calamity together."

Rhonna eyed them. "Since the first day you wound up on my farm, I knew. I knew you were special. I did my best by both of you to prepare you for whatever was coming. That time has come, and now you better be ready because I have a feeling that the fate of the world lies in the pairs of your hands."

41

The inner core of Dwarf Skull was a marvel of dwarven engineering. Similar to Dark Mountain, the city was built in and around the natural rocks that made up the plateau's landscape. Bridges made of iron girders stretched from one pinnacle to another. Some were wide enough for large carts and wagons, and the others were pedestrian walkways.

A network of tunnels weaved through the black rock, twisting and turning from balcony to walkway ledges with slides that led straight back down. Like a hive, there was level after level of cave mouths that led into pods where the dwarves and many others lived.

From the peak where Grey Cloak stood with his friends, he watched the dwarves bustle along like bearded worker ants from workstation to workstation. Their faces were grim, and they spoke little. Among them were many of the other races, keeping busy but with long faces as well. The spirit of Dwarf Skull appeared to be broken.

"It wasn't always this way," Rhonna said as she puffed on a cigar. She was still escorted by two dwarven soldiers in black helms that led them up to one of the smaller peaks overlooking the city. She'd made it a point to use discretion in their travels. She didn't want anyone to know that the blood brothers were there. "My kin are more robust and jollier, on occasion. Fierce fighters when the time comes, always prepared to battle. They enjoy training. When we lost so many of my family, well—" She blew out a stream of smoke. "Their spirits were darkened."

"We'll find a way," Grey Cloak said.

"Yes, well, don't get cocky. You don't have the Figurine of Doodads to bail your elven fanny out anymore. You'll have to use the gifts you were given." She tapped her temple. "And your wit. You have that. Use it. No more short-cuts. The journey will be long, and there is no easy way out." She looked out over her people and shook her head. "Never thought I'd see the day."

With his hands on the iron railing, Dyphestive said, "Has anyone else tried to stop Black Frost?"

"Word of smaller rebellions reaches us from time to time. If they become problematic, Black Frost sends fire from the sky," she said.

"You mean dragons?"

"No small rebellion stands a chance against an army of dragons, which," Rhonna remarked, "is much larger than when you left. It's rumored that Black Frost's forces hold most of the dragon charms and have been enslaving more dragons for the last decade. Now that his army has full control of the skies, he appears invincible."

Grey Cloak's slender fingers drummed the railing as he spied the people down below. They were miserable and scared thanks to Black Frost keeping a thumb on them, and everything had happened because of his gaffe. "All I wanted was to live life on my own terms, and now no one can, all because of one fat-arse dragon."

Dyphestive chuckled.

Rhonna's grim expression brightened. "It sounds like you're ready. I'll give you all the supplies you need for the journey, but I can't come, as much as I wish I could. I have tens of thousands to look after, and we have to be ready for Black Frost to stick his talon in our eye." She blew a smoke ring. "He enjoys reminding us that he's in control from time to time and usually will cut off our water supply. If I could, I'd send some of my finest dwarves with you, but I feel it's best that you travel alone."

"Agreed."

"Where will you go?" she asked.

"I think it's best if I don't say what I have in mind."

She nodded.

"Also, it seems that others don't fare so well in our

company," Grey Cloak said. "It seems the farther from us they stay, the better."

"No, you're being too hard on yourself." Rhonna gave him a tight hug around his waist. "As hardheaded as you are, you understand the most important matter."

"What's that?" he asked.

"Freedom and the price you have to pay for it."

HOURS LATER, Grey Cloak and Dyphestive were back out on the dusty trail, heading north with Dwarf Skull fading in the distance. It was the two of them and a pack mule in tow. "Rhonna really went all out for us, didn't she? An entire mule," Grey Cloak said, fanning his nose, "that smells like manure."

Dyphestive scratched the mule behind the ears. "I like him. And look at all this gear." The mule was gray with black-and-brown spots peppering his coat. He had a leather harness and a rope to tie him by and was loaded down with saddlebags, waterskins, and other traveling gear, such as blankets, sacks of dried fruit, meat, and bread. "I think this is the best equipped we've ever been to do anything. Tell me, where are we going? Shouldn't you have told Rhonna?"

"The less she knows, the better," Grey Cloak said. "People think we're ghosts, and we need to stay that way, so we'll have to be very careful, especially since you're as big as a horse. I don't think there's even a haystack big enough to hide you."

Dyphestive let out a jolly laugh. His voice was rich and robust. "I make a great target, but look." He tapped the breastplate on his chest. It had a dark, leathery veneer, but it was made of dwarven iron. "I have this."

"It looks heavy."

"No, not at all. And I don't know how she acquired it, but did you see my sword?" A sheathed two-handed sword was tied down to the pack mule. "It's the iron sword I acquired from the goblin chieftains. I thought I'd never see it again. She said she did some work on it. That's no surprise, seeing as she's a smith."

Grey Cloak's long strides stirred up the dust at his feet. "Well, you can't be hauling that around where we're going, so keep it packed up unless we need it."

"So, where are we going?" Dyphestive asked.

"Where this mess all began."

Dyphestive arched an eyebrow. "Dark Mountain?"

Grey Cloak shook his head. "No, Raven Cliff."

The big youth nodded. "Cliff."

"What?"

"Cliff," Dyphestive repeated. "That's what I'm naming the mule, Cliff." He scratched the mule behind the ears. "Hello, Cliff. How are you?"

Grey Cloak rolled his eyes.

42

It was midday, leagues south of the Iron Hills, and Grey Cloak stood on the edge of a riverbed. The river that once raced through the southern valleys had trickled down to little more than an ankle-deep stream. Dyphestive was bent over, filling the waterskins, while Grey Cloak looked out for enemies. He checked the skies. It had been days since he'd seen Streak, and he was worried.

Dyphestive slung the waterskins over his broad shoulders and loaded them back onto the mule, Cliff, who lapped up water from the river. "No sign of him, huh?" he asked.

"No," Grey Cloak said as he tapped his fingers on the pommel of his sword. "It's not like him either. Whatever help he went for must have been very far away."

"Can he find you?"

Grey Cloak shrugged. "We have a connection, and I think so, but I can't be sure. There's nothing but dead space up here. Nothing thrives, even with the water." He scanned the northern pathway of the river. It flowed straight into the distant Iron Hills. "It's no wonder Rhonna's people are so miserable. Did she say that Black Frost built dams to slow the flow?"

Dyphestive chucked a handful of dry branches into the water. "She did. They need a river flowing again, or they'll starve, won't they?"

"Only if they don't move, and I have a feeling the dwarves will starve before they move." He started north along the Twin Rivers path. "I think we should take a look."

Dyphestive towed Cliff along. "At the dam?"

"Exactly."

Dyphestive grinned. "You want to bust it open, don't you?"

Grey Cloak shrugged. "It's the least we can do for Rhonna after all she's been through. The trick is to do it so they don't blame the dwarves. It will have to look like an accident."

"It sounds dangerous."

Grey Cloak smirked. "I love danger. Don't you?"

Dyphestive gave a firm nod. "It's addictive."

THE BLOOD BROTHERS approached the dam just after night-fall and spied on it from a distance. It was a well-fortified structure made from logs and stone, built right against the backdrop of the jagged Iron Hills.

On the ground, on both sides of the river, were man-made canvas tents, enough to hold a score of troops. Soldiers in Black Guard armor—crimson tunics over chainmail—stood watch along the riverbeds while others ate by the evening bonfires.

The dam itself wasn't the most complex structure. The water followed caves that ran through the Iron Hills. Huge logs dammed up an opening from one side of the river to the other. The river itself was no more than fifty feet wide. The face of the dam was made up of logs stacked on top of logs, with small spaces in between that let the water flow through freely.

"You stay here with your friend Cliff. I'm going in for a closer look," Grey Cloak said.

Dyphestive nodded.

Grey Cloak took off into the shadows of the hills on the east side of the river, flanking the dam. The score of soldiers didn't appear to be a very strong force to guard a key strategical location. *There has to be more here than ordinary men. I could probably take them all out blindfolded—no, most likely—er, definitely.*

He navigated to the base of the hills only a hundred yards from the dam itself and began the climb. It was possible that the Black Guard was supremely confident that no one would challenge them, hence the smaller force, but it seemed unlikely.

Something else must be here.

Using the trees and rocks for cover, Grey Cloak crept toward the back side of the dam.

What do we have here?

Much like a castle, the wall behind the dam had a wooden walkway with another dozen soldiers positioned there. They were armed with crossbows and swords. Behind them, where the river spilled out of the hills, a pool of calm water gathered and swelled to the top of the cave mouth.

Grey Cloak sawed his finger over his chin. *Hmmm... how do I destroy the dam and make it look like an accident?*

He narrowed his eyes and inspected the crudely made structure. Though sound in design, the logs that made the dam's walls were bracketed in by more logs. If any of the logs on the edges gave way, the dam would collapse. The problem was the logs weighed tons, and moving them would be impossible.

He watched the soldiers behind the dam wall milling about. They were an assortment of men, orcs, and gnolls.

And how on earth do I distract so many witnesses?

As quiet as a deer, he slipped back to the hiding spot where Dyphestive and Cliff were waiting. He snuck up on Dyphestive and tapped him on the shoulder.

Dyphestive spun around and chopped a dagger over Grey Cloak's ducking head. "Don't spook me like that. I could have taken your head off."

"Not at that speed."

Dyphestive shook his head gently and sheathed his dagger. "I'm surprised you made it back without creating a commotion. What did you find?"

"There's another squad of soldiers behind the dam wall. Nothing else."

Giving Grey Cloak an eager look, Dyphestive said, "We can take them."

"I know, but we have to make it look like an accident. Like ghosts, we have to get in and out without being seen in case there are survivors."

"How do we do that?"

Grey Cloak's fingertips brightened with blue fire. "I have an idea."

43

With Dyphestive on the lookout, Grey Cloak headed back into the Iron Hills behind the dam. He crept back to the position that he'd stopped before and crouched in the rocks.

This might be my worst idea ever, but I'll take my chances.

He ran his fingers along the outer seam of the Cloak of Legends. It had been a long time since he'd taken advantage of its powers. Back when he'd been on Gunder Island, Anya had battled Riskers in the sky. He'd fallen into Lake Flugen, but thanks to the cloak's powers, he'd swum underneath the waters and breathed like a fish.

I can only assume it still works. Regardless. Grey Cloak took a breath and held it. From his perch, he dove into the deep pool of dammed-up water blocking the entrance of the cave. His body slipped into the dark waters like a knife without making a splash.

Brrr... colder than I thought.

In a few moments, he made it to the bottom of the pool, where the logs were bracketed in. He looked up where the moonlight shimmered above the waters and waited. He expected to see torches, possibly someone investigating his entrance, but it appeared that no one had caught on to his invasion.

Perfect.

His lungs started to burn, and he let out his breath. Air bubbled up through the water, and he breathed. Not only that, but his vision cleared.

Cloak of Legends, you are amazing.

Life had been so hectic that he'd never had the time to experiment with the cloak's powers. It wrapped him up like a warm blanket. He could breathe underwater and swim like a fish. There were many pockets, and he was able to float to the ground like a leaf. He'd discovered all of those powers out of desperation or by accident.

Now I have to do what I have to do on my own.

He took another look up through the waters. He was at least twelve feet below the surface and underneath the catwalks where the Black Guard was stationed. He called forth his wizardry fire.

His hands ignited in blue flame. The waters began to bubble and simmer.

Yuri Gnomeknower had warned him about the dangers of using the wizard fire without an object. It could burn his hands to a crisp like hers. But by his own inspiration, he'd found that doing it underwater didn't burn at all.

Yes! My fingertips aren't burning to a crisp.

Summoning more mystic energy, he started to burn the underwater brackets at the weakest link.

It's working! Yes, it's working! I wish Yuri were still around to see this.

FROM HIS HIDING SPOT, Dyphestive felt invisible fingers crawling up his spine. Goose bumps popped up on his arms as he watched the pool of black water. He could see a murky blue-green glow deep beneath the surface. A surge of tiny bubbles rose.

Holy Horseshoes, how long can he hold his breath?

But out of the corner of his eye, he caught sight of something long slithering over the surface of the water. It dove deep.

Grey Cloak, look out!

GREY CLOAK SAWED deep into the wooden brackets. The first beam cracked and bowed.

Suddenly, the Cloak of Legends flexed around his body.

He turned and found himself face-to-face with a twenty-foot-long dragon snake. It was a hideous thing with the face of a dragon and fins on its head. Built like a snake, it still had four small legs for crawling. He'd seen dragon snakes in Dark Mountain before, crawling among the rocks.

Hello, hideous one. Grey Cloak blasted fire from his fingertips. It was too late.

The dragon snake rammed him into the brackets and knocked the breath out of him.

DYPHESTIVE RAN toward the pool of water with a full head of steam. He tried to be as quiet as he could, but the blood rushing behind his ears drowned out everything else.

The Black Guard spotted him and started pointing and shouting, "Intruder! Intruder!"

The crossbowmen took aim and fired the first volley just as Dyphestive dove.

A crossbow bolt lodged into the meat of his shoulder a split second before he splashed down and sank like a stone.

THE DRAGON SNAKE coiled its serpentine body around Grey Cloak like a python and started to squeeze.

He wormed his arms out of the watery coils of the dragon snake just in time and drove his burning thumbs into its eyes. With a monstrous spasm, the dragon snake's body flexed, loosened, and tightened again.

Zooks! It's squeezing me to death!

Grey Cloak poured out all the firepower he had left, but his burning hands were extinguished. His ribs started to snap.

Ugh! I don't want to die in a watery grave.

The dragon snake lifted him above the water, where he saw the Black Guard pointing and looking at him. They were all packed on the dam's walkway. *Perfect.* He gave them a wink and wave of his fingers.

The monster plunged him back underneath the water and dragged him to the muddy bottom, where it held him fast. It applied more pressure. Another rib popped. Grey Cloak's vision started to dim, and even with the cloak, he couldn't breathe.

Out of nowhere, a black hulk appeared and locked the dragon snake's head in tree-trunk arms.

Dyphestive!

The brawny youth jammed a dagger deep into the monster's gills. It flexed and released Grey Cloak. Dyphestive held on for his life with one arm locked around the dragon serpent's neck and the other stabbing away.

The bleeding serpent thrashed underneath the waters, slipped free of Dyphestive's grasp, and disappeared into the cave. Dyphestive swam upward and burst through the water's surface.

Grey Cloak swam after his brother with his cracked ribs burning like fire. He popped up out of the water. The first thing he saw was the arrow sticking out of his brother's shoulder. "You're wounded."

"I've had worse." A crossbow bolt sang by Dyphestive's nose and sank into the waters. "Not that I'm inviting any more."

The Black Guard shouted at them with torches in hand and crossbows firing. "Surrender! Surrender!" they shouted.

"Can you hold your breath long?" Grey Cloak asked.

"Longer than you."

"Follow me under. We're going to need your muscle to finish this, and don't forget to use your legs." Grey Cloak dove. With Dyphestive on his tail, he led them to the brackets that held the dam in place. He managed enough fire in his hands to create soft light in the depths.

Dyphestive looked right at him with his cheeks puffed out. Grey Cloak showed him the scarring on the wooden beams he'd blasted into with his hands. Dyphestive nodded. He grabbed the bracket, set his feet on the base, and heaved.

Grey Cloak gave his brother a thumbs-up the moment

he heard the beams pop. He swam back to the surface, waded in the pool, and faced the Black Guard.

"I surrender. I surrender!" he said.

A Black Guard carrying a torch said, "Get out of there, elf!"

One thing was for certain. There was no way they would come to get him, not loaded down with all their heavy armor. Grey Cloak smirked as he counted bodies. Over thirty soldiers were on the dam's platform, and he had no doubt that was all of them. He lifted his hands and waved. "I'm coming." He swam for the bank.

A loud pop exploded beneath the surface. The dam's platform buckled, and the eastern bracket collapsed. From the bottom up, the dam gave way. The platform fell into the rushing waters with all of the soldiers on it. Each and every one of them sank like an anchor and disappeared underneath the waves.

Grey Cloak made it to the bank before the waters swept him away. He wasn't alone either. Dyphestive was crawling for his life up the rocks with the waters rushing over his ankles. They were both puffing for breath as they reunited and watched the waters take the dam's logs and drowning soldiers to a watery grave.

Dyphestive sat on the rocks and pulled the bolt free of his shoulder. "Great plan."

"I couldn't have done it without you." Grey Cloak smiled, clasped his brother's hands, and helped him to his feet. "It was the least we could do for Rhonna. And she shouldn't get blamed. It looks like the perfect accident."

"Like I said, great plan."

The dragon snake's head burst out of the waters and rose above the blood brothers. It came at them.

Dyphestive had his back to the monster as he looked into his brother's eyes. He reached into Grey Cloak's cloak, snatched his sword from its scabbard, and turned his hips in a violent backswing. The blade cut the dragon serpent's head clean off. It flew upward, came down, bounced off the rocks, and was taken with the waters.

Without giving the monster a glance, Dyphestive slid Grey Cloak's sword back into its sheath and said, "Thanks."

Grey Cloak tossed back his head and erupted with jubilant laughter.

44

IRON HILLS

That same night, the blood brothers navigated through the rocky woodland of the Iron Hills and made a small campfire. It was a cloudy pitch-black night shaded with great pines whose branches whistled and bent in the wind.

Grey Cloak warmed his hands over the little fire's flickering flames. "How is the shoulder?"

Rolling his wounded shoulder without so much as a grimace, Dyphestive replied, "Not bad. How are your ribs?"

"Could be better." Grey Cloak quickly learned that if he breathed too deeply, it felt like someone was stabbing his chest with a knife. Meanwhile, he chewed on a dried hunk of meat the size of his hand. "You know what I think?"

Dyphestive swallowed a hunk of meat whole. "What?"

"I think we're getting pretty good at being heroes. That's

what I think. You took that dragon snake's head off without even seeing it. Impressive."

Dyphestive grinned. "I did, didn't I?"

Grey Cloak nodded. "It was impressive, the work of heroes."

"It sounds to me like you've had a change of heart. What about fortune and glory?"

Grey Cloak lay back on the ground. "As long as I have enough to live on when I'm old, I'll survive. Perhaps we can live like Crane and join the Brotherhood of Whispers. They appear to have it good."

"At the rate we are going, we might not make it to a respectable age."

Grey Cloak propped himself up on one elbow. "Whatever do you mean? Look at us. Ten years have passed, and we haven't aged a day. We look great. Well, at least I do."

Dyphestive stuck his big chin out and nodded. "Grey, I honestly feel like we can do anything. Is that awful?"

Grey Cloak flipped his hand out and said, "I think that comes with being a natural. And remember we aren't the only ones that feel this way. There are others."

"So, you feel the same way too?"

"I've always felt... invincible." Grey Cloak picked up a small branch and flicked it into the fire. "Even when I was young. That's why I hated Dark Mountain so much. At least, that's one reason. I never felt the others, like Dirklen and Magnolia, were any better than me."

"They're ten years older now. Won't they be stronger?"

"I suppose, but we're stronger too. Ten years or no. We can take those pampered worm riders any day."

Dyphestive cracked his neck side to side and managed a smile, but it vanished when he said, "Do you believe Anya's dead?"

"She's too stubborn. I'll believe it when I see it. Listen, brother, we're going to find a way to make it all right."

"I thought we could use the time mural again and go back," Dyphestive remarked. "That would fix everything."

"I've thought the same thing, but it would take a miracle to get near a time mural again. Not to mention, no one has any control over it." Grey Cloak lay flat on his back and stared up at the branches. He'd already thought about using the time mural, but he couldn't see how he could use something that he wouldn't be able to control. "We'll find answers in Raven Cliff. With any luck, Tanlin is still around." He rolled over on one side. "Get some rest, brother. I have a feeling we're going to need it."

"Agreed."

45

The blood brothers neared the top of the Iron Hills, traversing the rocks and ridges with little problem. The bright sun shone through the leaves while the varmints and birds hustled through the branches.

Dyphestive towed Cliff behind him. The mule's passage had been steady until then. From the higher ground, Grey Cloak looked back and saw Cliff stopped on the trail.

Dyphestive was pulling the pack beast's harness and saying, "Come, Cliff. Come."

"What's the matter?" Grey Cloak asked as he made his way down the hill.

"He won't move," Dyphestive said.

"Well, make him."

Dyphestive looked at Grey Cloak like he was stupid and handed him the rope. "You make him."

"Fine, I'll show you how it's done." He pulled on the mule's rope. "Time to go, mule." His boots slid over the ground as he pulled, but Cliff wouldn't budge. The only things that moved on the mule were his ears and his tail, which flapped at the flies. "This is ridiculous. What did you do to him?"

"Nothing. He stopped." Dyphestive scratched Cliff behind the ears. "Maybe he's tired."

"He's a mule. They don't get tired, at least not after this short of a trip. Pinch him or something."

"I'm not going to pinch him."

"Well, you have to do something. We're almost to the top. It's all—"

"It's all what?" Dyphestive asked.

Grey Cloak lifted his hand to signal for silence. He'd caught a glimpse of yellow eyes in the bushes. It was a goblin. He knew it the instant he saw him. "We're being followed," he said under his breath. "Goblins. I can hear one running through the woodland now. We need to go, Dyphestive. We need to hurry."

A wild cry came up from the hollows of the woodland. It was the savage call of the goblins and their hounds.

"Come on, Cliff. Come on!" Dyphestive pleaded as he pulled on the harness.

Cliff pulled his neck back and brayed.

"Leave him," Grey Cloak said as he started up the hill. "We can outrun them, but we have to go now!"

"I'm not leaving him," Dyphestive said.

"Are you out of your skull? You'll get us both killed over a worthless mule. Don't you remember the last time we crossed the goblins in these hills? They would have killed all of us if not for the figurine, and I don't have that now."

"I don't care," Dyphestive said. "I'm not leaving Cliff behind."

Grey Cloak's eyes grew to the size of saucers. He couldn't believe his eyes. Dyphestive stooped underneath Cliff the mule, and setting his jaw, he lifted the beast onto his shoulders.

"What in the wild, wild woodland are you doing?"

Dyphestive started up the hill with hundreds of pounds of living mule flesh on his shoulders. "Wherever I go, Cliff goes too."

Grey Cloak smirked. "You're crazy."

Up the hill they went at a brisk pace, as fast as Dyphestive's long strides would take him. The mule, loaded down with gear, didn't slow him at all. His sure feet plowed through the low-hanging branches and prickly brush.

"So much for moving with discretion," Grey Cloak said. He could hear the goblin horde coming.

Their shrill voices demanded the blood of the enemy that invaded their forest. Their hungry hounds sped forward, barking and howling wildly.

"Move faster!"

To his surprise, they made it to the bald knob at the top

of the hill and raced over the long stretch of grass to the other side.

We might make it. I can't believe we might make it.

He sped out ahead of Dyphestive and came to an abrupt stop at the rim of the hill. Another force of goblins, scores of them, raced up the other side. He pointed east. "That way! That way!"

They made it another twenty yards and stopped.

Zooks!

The goblin horde had hemmed them in from all directions.

46

The goblin horde consisted of a bunch of dirty little men—rank with filthy, greasy, matted hair, covered in furs and skins—who carried crude weapons. Their bright-yellow eyes were hooded by their knitted brows, and their tattooed and pierced faces were visages of evil.

They held their wild dogs by collars and chains, and the slavering beasts barked and howled.

Dyphestive lowered Cliff to the ground while Grey Cloak drew his swords from their sheaths. They stood back-to-back beside the mule, listening to the goblins' wild howling.

A loud voice rose above the noise. "Silence!"

The goblins fell silent, and a knot of the grungy little men parted and took a knee.

A huge goblin that towered over the others approached

from the other side of the hill from where Grey Cloak and Dyphestive had come. It was the goblin chieftain, similar to the one they'd met before but bigger. His shock of hair was shaved on both sides, and iron hoop earrings hung in a chain from his ears. His nose was broad and flat. Coarse black hairs covered his oily body. He was deep chested and had a barrel of a belly. Muscles bulged beneath a healthy layer of fat. On his shoulder, he carried a wooden club with metal spikes driven through the head.

"He looks reasonable," Grey Cloak said. "Let me do the talking." He cleared his throat. "Ahem. Mighty chieftain, we desire safe and peaceful passage through the Iron Hills and would be very grateful if you granted it."

The goblin chieftain's nostrils widened, and his chest heaved as he locked his eyes on Dyphestive and his sword. "You!" he bellowed. "Where did you get that sword?"

Dyphestive glanced at Grey Cloak and whispered, "Should I answer that? Because I don't think he's going to like the answer."

Grey Cloak shook his head and turned his attention to the hulking goblin chieftain. He was very much the same as the goblin that Venir the Darkslayer had slain years ago. Scores of goblins had died that day. Perhaps it was the right time to remind them of it. "Over ten years ago, I traveled with a group that had a run-in with two goblin chieftains. They carried tremendous clubs, similar to what you carry. As a matter of fact, I believe that club is the very same."

The goblin chieftain dropped his club from his shoulder with an uneasy look. He sneered at Grey Cloak. "One of those chieftains was my father." He twirled the massive club over his wrists with ease. "I saw the carnage. I smelled the blood. I kneeled over my father's corpse and vowed vengeance—if I ever found the man, or elf, who did that to my people, I would kill him." He pointed his club at Grey Cloak. "And now, you admit this crime to me." He lifted his club high overhead. "I am Jubax! I call for blood! I call for vengeance! By the word of Jubax, goblin chieftain, king of the Iron Hills, I will have it! We will have it!"

The goblins erupted in wild howls.

Grey Cloak backed toward his brother.

Raising his voice above the crowd, Dyphestive said, "Maybe you shouldn't have told them that we killed his father."

"You think? I was trying to intimidate him." He rummaged through his pockets.

"What is the opposite of intimidate?" Dyphestive snapped his fingers. "Incite! Are you sure that wasn't what you were trying to do?"

"Gum up!" Grey Cloak pulled out one of the carvings he'd made of the Figurine of Heroes from one of the Cloak of Legends's many pockets. He placed it on the ground for all the goblins to see and lifted his hands like a great wizard.

Jubax and the goblins dropped their eyes to the face of the figurine and fell silent.

Grey Cloak shouted, "I warn you! By the power of my figurine, all of your filthy brethren were destroyed. I will use it again, and even more of you will perish." He pointed at them one by one. "You! You! You! And you!"

The goblins stepped back and cowered.

"What will it be, Jubax?" Grey Cloak asked. "Will you take another treacherous step and eradicate the goblins from these hills forever, or will you be wise and back away?"

Jubax's chest heaved, and his nostrils flared as his forehead wrinkled in many layers. His gaze switched between Grey Cloak, the iron sword, and the figurine. "I gave my word as a son, now as a king. I won't break it whether you summon your witchcraft or not." He glowered at Grey Cloak and lifted his club. "Prepare to die!"

As the goblins moved in, Grey Cloak snatched up the false figurine, charged it with wizardry, and hurled it at Jubax.

Jubax swung his club at the figurine and hit it squarely. The figurine blew up, and it knocked Jubax backward as he stumbled and fell over his feet.

Grey Cloak joined his brother. "That could've gone better."

"Two bad bluffs. Do you care to go for three?" Dyphestive asked as he tightened his grip on his sword and swung at the nearest goblin. The blade sliced the fiendish man in half.

"I had to try, and you didn't have any ideas at all that I can recall." Grey Cloak's two quick sword strokes felled two more goblins.

"You didn't give me a chance." Dyphestive stepped forward and lanced two goblins with his sword. He pushed their bodies free with his boot. "But I didn't have any better ideas. I thought yours were really good."

Jubax climbed back to his feet, and with a murderous look in his eye, his shouted, "I want their skulls! Kill them!"

Launching powerful, arcing swings, Dyphestive hewed ranks of goblins down in threes and fours.

Grey Cloak charged his swords with wizard fire, turning the steel into bright-blue flames. Dancing, dodging, and striking, he pierced the goblin enemy, one heart after the next.

The wild foes piled up, but they kept on coming, spurred on by their chieftain, Jubax.

"Kill them! Kill them!"

"There's only one way to do this," Dyphestive said as he skewered a goblin and flung it off his sword. "Go after Jubax!"

"Agreed," Grey Cloak said as his blade bit deep into the neck of a goblin. He stabbed another in the heart with his short sword. "But there are waves of them." Grey Cloak made as quick work of the goblins as he could, but more and more of them rose up over the hills. It took every ounce of skill and strength he could muster to fend off the filthy minions. "There're too many! Any ideas?"

Dyphestive replied as he busted a goblin's teeth with his fist, "Do you remember what Venir the Darkslayer said?"

"No!"

A goblin jumped on Dyphestive's back and tried to crack his head open with a leg bone. Dyphestive grinned as he dropped his sword and flung the goblin into the horde. "Fight or die!"

47

The goblin forces poured over the blood brothers like a wave of angry ants. They didn't have skill, but they had numbers.

Slice! Pop! Glitch! Stab! Chop! Thunk! Slice!

The unfettered horde chased after Grey Cloak as he slid to freedom and brought quick death, time after time. His sore ribs burned like fire, and his arms became heavy. The glow in his swords dimmed, and he fought on, brawn against brawn.

A pack of goblin war dogs knifed through the surge and pounced. Their bodies crashed into Grey Cloak's. He slipped and went down.

Zooks!

A dog bit down on his arm. Another tore and yanked at

his cloak with slavering teeth. He kicked one dog in the jaw.

"Get off me!" He let go of his swords and switched to his daggers. A war dog yelped when he cut into its ribs.

The goblins came, reckless and wild-eyed, to pile on.

A blaring dragon roar exploded in the sky that put a halt to everything.

"ROOOOOOOOAAAAAAAARRR!"

The cowering goblins dared a skyward look.

Fire from the sky came down with a mighty wrath. Dragon fire burned their dark, oily bodies to crisps. Burnt hair and scorched animal skins brought the sweet aroma of death. Goblins burned, dropped, and rolled.

Grey Cloak pushed out of the pile of panic-stricken fiends. "Streak!"

The runt dragon landed on the ground, spitting a geyser of flames. He wasn't alone.

"Eeeee-yaaaaaah!" an army of quarry gnomes screamed. They poured out of the woodland with hammers and picks in hand. The stocky miners—with pointed beards, leather aprons, and metal caps—blasted into the shocked goblins' ranks.

JUBAX SHOOK WITH RAGE. "No! No!" He brained a gnome with his club and turned his wrath loose on another.

Smash!

The quarry gnome, shorter than a goblin but stouter, was pulverized.

The goblin chieftain dropped his club and slipped a pair of iron knuckles over his fingers. He pointed at Dyphestive. "I'll have my family's sword back."

Dyphestive stabbed the sword into the ground. "Come and take it!"

Jubax strolled across the battlefield. Towering over Dyphestive, he said, "You killed my father. You killed my uncles." Jubax slammed his huge fists together with a *clang*.

"I didn't kill any of them, but on behalf of the warrior who did—" Dyphestive balled up his fists. "Let's dan—"

Jubax punched him in the jaw so hard it spun him around.

Dyphestive's knees wobbled, and he fell to a knee, his ears ringing. He rubbed his jaw and spit blood. "Let's try this again."

The goblin chieftain rained down hammering blows, his big fists colliding with Dyphestive's body. He pounded the big youth down like a hammer driving a spike. "You will die! You will die!"

Dyphestive absorbed all the punishment he could take. He turned into Jubax's body and socked him in the ribs. The crack of bone followed, and Jubax fell backward like a tree. The goblin was dead.

Dyphestive looked at his fist and muttered, "I only hit him once."

"Don't flatter yourself." Grey Cloak wiped his bloody sword off on Jubax's body.

"You killed him?"

"A quick jab to the pumper. We don't have time for you to dance with the goblins." Grey Cloak sheathed his sword. "So of course I killed him. We have things to do."

Dyphestive shook his head in disbelief. He wanted to fight, but the fight was over. With the death of Jubax and the arrival of the quarry gnomes, the remainder of the goblin force scattered like rats. He caught sight of a quarry gnome saluting him with a hammer. He was the last of the living that vanished into the woodland.

As quickly as the battle had started, it ended, leaving a field of food for the crows, some still roasting.

GREY CLOAK FOUND Streak perched on Cliff's back, licking the mule's ears. How the mule had survived, he didn't know, but he was elated to see his dragon again. "Streak! You couldn't have shown up at a better time!" He hugged the thickly built dragon and started to pet him. "Where have you been?"

"Getting help, like Dyphestive told me to," Streak

replied in the sly but polished manner of a well-spoken child. "Good help is hard to come by these days."

"You can say that again," Grey Cloak said. His heart was still racing, and he caught his breath. He noticed Dyphestive looking at Streak with wide eyes. "What?"

Approaching the dragon and mule, Dyphestive fingered his ear. "Did Streak speak?"

Grey Cloak stiffened. He and Streak had a connection that allowed them to communicate, but it wasn't vocal speech, rather more like a sense of understanding. "You heard that?" he asked Dyphestive.

"My ears are ringing so loud, I'm not sure."

"Streak," Grey Cloak asked the dragon, "did you speak?"

Streak's pink tongue probed the mule's ears. He licked his nose and Grey Cloak's cheek. "Who is this fellow?" he asked, eyeing the mule. "I don't recall him being a part of the group. I bet he's tasty."

Wide-eyed, Grey Cloak snatched Streak off the saddle and held him at arm's length. "Streak, you can talk?"

As stiff as a board, Streak eyed Grey Cloak. "Of course I can. Which is more than I can say of this mule." He nodded. "How have you been?"

Grey Cloak nodded excitedly. "Better."

"I'm glad to see that you are well. I was worried about you, and I went for help"—he turned his thick lizard neck in Dyphestive's direction—"as your brother insisted. On my journey, I had a delay."

"What sort of delay?" Dyphestive asked.

"A deep slumber overcame me. I can't really explain it, but I think it had something to do with that silver fish that I ate. I'll tell you, I've felt fabulous since I consumed it." He exchanged glances with both men. "You remember the silver fish, don't you?"

"The one in the Wizard Watch fountain?" Dyphestive asked.

"The very one. I got him." Streak smiled, revealing a mouthful of sharp teeth. "Needless to say, the rest did me some good, and I immediately tracked you down. That's when I discovered the quarry gnomes and found my tongue. You should have seen their faces when I spoke to them. They fell down and worshipped me. Literally, but I bade them to follow orders and attack the goblins who were on your trail. Hence here we are."

Grey Cloak and Dyphestive exchanged uncertain looks.

That was when Grey Cloak noticed a few details about Streak that he'd overlooked. Small horns had popped up on the dragon's face, and the ridges on his back had hardened, not to mention he was noticeably bigger. He pet his dragon with a happy look on his face. "So now I have a talking, and flying, fire-breathing dragon. What more could an elf ask for?"

"Stick around," Streak said. "I'm full of surprises."

48

RAVEN CLIFF

I t was pouring rain by early evening when they entered the city of Raven Cliff. The cobblestone streets ran with water. Citizens dashed from porch to porch, seeking cover, while others trudged along the streets, submitting to the pounding rain.

Water flowed down from the steeply slanted roofs of the buildings and made huge puddles. Refuse floated underneath the porches and flooded into the grates in the alleys.

A group of children chased a boat made from a block of wood down the road, their bare feet splashing in the water. The boat came to a stop at a soldier's feet, where the water pooled around his boots. He was a Black Guard in full gear. He bent over, picked up the boat, and chucked it down the road.

The children scattered.

Grey Cloak and Dyphestive avoided eye contact with the harsh-looking soldier and moved along.

"Zooks, there are Black Guards everywhere. What happened to this place?" Grey Cloak asked.

"Ten years of Black Frost, I suppose," Dyphestive commented.

Grey Cloak had liked Raven Cliff the first time he'd come there. It had been a thriving city, bustling with excitement and adventure. The people had been forthcoming and amiable, and there had been plenty to do and see. It was where he'd chased Zora down and become a member of Talon. It was also the place where Dalsay, Adanadel, and Browning had died. It was where he'd lost his brother to the Doom Riders too. It appeared that the dark times had become darker.

A dragon shrieked above the streets.

The citizens cowered.

A middling dragon perched on one of the rooftops. It launched into the sky and shrieked again.

"Zooks, where there are dragons, there are bound to be Riskers," Grey said as he pushed Streak's head down into the bundles Cliff carried. "Keep low. We can't let anyone see you."

Streak flicked his tongue out and sniffed. "Something smells good."

"Agreed," Dyphestive said as he patted his stomach.

"They have great meals here, and I'm tired of dried meat. I want something fresh, plates of butter-baked bread, strips of bacon, turkey legs, potatoes."

Grey Cloak hungered himself. "Let's find a place to stay. Come on. I remember a few places that should be suitable."

He found a run-down tavern on the edge of town and stabled Cliff. "What do you want to do, Streak? You might be too big to go unnoticed now."

"I'll keep Cliff company. Besides, I saw some juicy barn cats prowling about. I think I'll venture out and meet them," Streak said.

"Low profile," Grey Cloak warned.

Streak flicked his tongue out.

The inside of the rickety tavern had more chairs than customers. Water ran down the chimney stack, but a fire was burning. The blood brothers took a table in the corner with full view of the front door.

A robust waitress approached. She had tired eyes and messy hair, and her apron was marred with food stains. "What can I do for you?"

"We need a room, two beds, a growler of ale, hot bread, a bowl of that stew I smell, and a plateful of your finest meat," Dyphestive said.

The waitress looked him up and down. "You'll need a big bed. I'll make it happen. I fix the food, and it might even come with an extra side of me." She walked away with her hips swaying.

"Try not to fall in love," Grey Cloak said. "We still have to locate your wife, Leena."

"She's not my wife." Dyphestive showed a weary look. "Do we have to find her? I hate to think of what she'll do to me after disappearing for ten years. Maybe she forgot and moved on."

"Maybe she's dead."

"Don't say that." Dyphestive dried his damp face with a cloth napkin. "When are we going to see Tanlin?"

"*We* aren't going to see Tanlin."

Dyphestive gave him a puzzled look. "What do you mean? That's why we're here, aren't we?"

"I'm going to find Tanlin by myself. We can't barge into his store and catch up on old times. First, we need to see if he's there, and second, there might be spies keeping an eye on him, and I'm not going to take any chances."

"But you always take chances."

"You know what I mean." The waitress returned with a growler of ale and moved back to the kitchen. "I'll exercise more caution this time. At this point, we can't trust anyone, Tanlin included."

49

The first thing Grey Cloak picked up on outside of
Tanlin's Fine Fittings and Embroidery was the
numerous Black Guard in the area. They were thickly gathered in one of the most active merchant streets in the entire
city and staring at struggling citizens with hawkish looks.

It was morning, one of the busiest times of the day, and
the hard rains had leveled down to a steady drizzle. Across
the street, Grey Cloak peered out from an alley where he
squatted down by a rain barrel, covered in his cloak.

Rain steadily dripped from the porch over Tanlin's
store, splashing into the potholes in the deteriorating
roads. The doors to Tanlin's store were closed, but fine
clothing on mannequins was on full display in front of the
windows.

Squeezed in between an eatery and a shoe shop,

Tanlin's store drew a constant flow of passersby. A woman in a big hat decorated with flowers stood outside Tanlin's door, tapping her foot and peeking in the window.

Where is he? He should be open by now. He always opened early before. I bet he's in the back working. Maybe I should check.

Finally, the front door opened inward, and Tanlin came into full view. He'd changed little. He was clean-shaven, with soft brown sculpted hair. He wore a pressed white button-down shirt, black slacks, and a purple scarf around his neck. Tanlin greeted the woman with a warm smile and stepped aside.

That was when Grey Cloak noticed the limp in Tanlin's stride and the cane the man carried in hand. Tanlin's face grimaced when he walked.

What happened to him?

Grey Cloak kept his eyes glued to Tanlin's store for the next few hours. Customers came and went, and he was careful to move from his spot and walk the streets with the crowd from time to time. The only person that stayed in the store with Tanlin was a pudgy woman who wore a knit cap on her head. Other than that, little changed.

Grey Cloak couldn't fight the feeling that something was amiss. The Black Guard hovered near Tanlin's store and kept a watchful eye through the window. They even sauntered in from time to time. One of the soldiers knocked a pile of shirts onto the floor and stepped on it.

The portly woman was quick to pick it up after the Black Guard left. Grey Cloak could see her bickering with Tanlin now and again.

Hmm, maybe he remarried.

Dusk came, and soon after, the doors to Tanlin's Fine Fittings and Embroidery closed.

Grey Cloak stole his way around to the alley behind the store, but something was still eating at him that he couldn't put his finger on. Rather than steal down the dark alley, he opted to climb to the rooftops instead. He glided over the slanted roofs and waited across the street.

Tanlin exited and locked the door behind him. His assistant was with him, her arm hooked in his, as he hobbled down the alley, cane clacking on the ground.

Grey Cloak was just about to follow when something flew out from underneath the building's eaves. His blood froze. *A yonder!*

The strange eyeball creature hovered in the air on bat wings for a moment then sailed silently after Tanlin.

Zooks, they're watching him! Why?

He followed Tanlin all the way to a small apartment complex only a few blocks from the store. Tanlin entered on the first level of the three-story building and vanished. The yonder floated outside then flew upward, stopping level with the top apartments. It attached itself to the building wall across the street and turned to stone.

He-he-he. I might not know what's going on, but I know

exactly where Tanlin lives. Now, for some patience. Well played, Grey Cloak, well played.

GREY CLOAK CHECKED in with Dyphestive and Streak and headed back to Tanlin's apartment the next day. He entered the apartment building, took the stairwell to the third floor, and put an ear to Tanlin's door.

All is quiet. Just the way I like it.

Scanning both sides of the hallway, he removed his thief's tools—two metal picks—and started picking the lock. He raked the small tumblers with one pick while applying pressure to the locking mechanism with the other.

I should have known it wouldn't be your standard lock.

One of the apartment doors down the hall opened.

Grey Cloak stopped picking the lock and casually acted like he was looking for a certain door. A fluffy white cat slunk out of the other apartment, and the door closed behind it.

Ah, close call.

He squatted down and said, "Here, kitty, kitty."

The cat with bright-green eyes sauntered over and rubbed up against his leg. It started to purr.

He picked up the cat. "You don't want to come home with me. My little dragon will make a meal of you." He set the cat down. "Now, hurry along before I change my mind."

The white cat scampered away and vanished down the stairwell.

Checking both ends of the hall, Grey Cloak resumed his lock picking. A few moments passed, and the latch popped. "There we go." He opened the door a crack, listened, and entered. When he closed the door behind him, he noticed a small dove feather lying on the floor. "Clever."

The feather was an old trick Tanlin had taught him. The feather was placed at the top of the door, inside the seam, after the door was locked. If someone entered, the feather would fall unnoticed, but Tanlin would know if someone was inside before he went in because the feather would no longer show in the door's seam where he'd placed it.

Grey Cloak put the feather back in place and made his way around the quaint and well-furnished apartment. Velvety burgundy curtains were drawn in front of the bay window. A single bedroom held twin beds, neatly made with blankets folded on the end. A comfortable sofa as well as tables and chairs for dining occupied the living room. The kitchen had cupboards mounted on the wall and a wardrobe that was too big for the small bedroom.

He put his hand over the coal-burning stove and felt the warmth rising from the metal plates. A half-filled canister of tea sat next to the stove with small china cups beside it.

I bet if I thoroughly searched this place, I'd find a heap of treasure. He eyed the nooks and crannies but thought better of it and moved to the curtains. Through the slit in the middle of the curtains, he could see the building across the street where the yonder had nestled the night before. It was gone. *A good thing.*

Grey Cloak stared out the window, waiting for nightfall.

Hours later, the same as the night before, Tanlin and his companion ambled down the back alleys. A yonder appeared and nestled under the building's eaves across the street. He tucked himself into the kitchen, out of sight from the exit.

A key fumbled at the lock. The latch popped, and the door swung open.

Grey Cloak peeked around the corner.

Tanlin entered, cane in hand, with a shorter woman filing in behind him. He closed the door, bent over, and picked up the feather. The woman hung their cloaks inside a small open closet beside the door. She took his cane and hung it by the handle on a peg. Together, they wandered inside. They froze the moment Grey Cloak slipped in front of them with his dagger blades on their throats.

"Shhhh," he said as he watched their eyes widen. "Shhhh... Zora?"

50

EPILOGUE

There was no mistaking Zora's beautiful eyes. Her cheeks were big and her face as round as a pie, but it was her, curves and all. Her petite build was gone, replaced with a fuller figure.

Grey Cloak wasn't the only one gawping. Tanlin and Zora looked at him with stupefied expressions, as if seeing a ghost. Their jaws hung open, and their eyes were wide with amazement. They appeared weary too. Tanlin's distinguished features had begun to sag, and he carried a fatigue about him. Zora, still beautiful, didn't have the same energetic luster in her eyes that she used to.

The tired-eyed Tanlin broke the silence, glanced at the blade on his throat, and said, "If you'll please, Grey Cloak."

"Oh, zooks, sorry." Grey Cloak tucked his weapons away. "I was being cautious."

"You broke into my place. Well done," Tanlin said with a thin smile.

"I learned from the—*oof*!"

Zora tackled him onto the sofa and peppered his face with kisses. She hugged and squeezed him tight. "I thought you were dead!"

"I'm not," he said quietly, "but keep your voice down. We're being watched."

Tanlin limped over to the curtains and peeked outside. "I know, a yonder. Bloody thing watches us like a hawk." He looked at Grey Cloak. "Are you sure it didn't see you?"

"Positive."

Zora still straddled him and kept him pinned down when he tried to stand.

He poked her chubby cheek. "What happened?"

She frowned. "My human side has gotten the better of me the last decade. Needless to say, I've found my only pleasure in eating since you've been gone."

"Are you saying I made you fat?" Grey Cloak asked.

"Yes." She grinned.

"Zora, stop playing games," Tanlin said as he ambled into the kitchen. "Let me put on some tea while we get caught up on past and present matters."

"Why are they watching you?" Grey Cloak asked as his hands settled on Zora's waist.

"They're watching for you and your brother," Tanlin said as he prepared the tea. "Is he alive?"

"He's fine. Hiding at the moment, at least I hope he is. Why are they looking for us? We've been gone a decade."

Tanlin spun a kitchen chair backward and sat down. He tapped his nose. "I'm still tapped into the Brotherhood of Whispers. As we understand it, you're still perceived as a threat. They want the Figurine of Heroes. It's those invaders, Catten and Verbard, who desire it. Tell us, what happened in Wizard Watch over a decade ago?"

"Well, it hasn't been so long for me. Not even a couple of weeks. But this is what happened." Grey Cloak told them every detail, from the battle inside the Wizard Watch to his meeting with Rhonna at Dwarf Skull. With a long face, he said, "I never would have imagined that I could make matters ten times worse than they were."

Zora climbed off him as he finished, but she still held his hand. "It's not all your fault. I mean, most of it is, but not all of it."

"Thanks, Zora. That makes me feel better."

The teapot whistled, and Tanlin hustled over to the stove.

Grey Cloak could see pain in the old man's tired eyes. "What happened to your leg?"

Tanlin prepared the cup and saucers of fine china. "A warning from Black Frost and his minions. The only reason Zora and I are still alive is because we've agreed to spy for them. Otherwise, we'd be imprisoned, the same as the rest of them." He handed Grey Cloak a cup of tea. "I should inform them that you're here, but I won't. We won't, of course." He sat back down.

Grey Cloak's back straightened. "Are you telling me that you work for Black Frost?"

"We serve the Brotherhood of Whispers, not Black Frost. Black Frost thinks we serve him, but we don't." Tanlin sipped his tea. "I have an arrangement that keeps us safe. It's with Baron Dorenzo, the ruler of Raven Cliff in name only. He's merely a puppet of the Black Guard now, but I check in with him for information. It keeps the Riskers off our backs."

"Riskers?"

Zora nodded. "Riskers and their dragons occupy every major city. They maintain the order throughout Gapoli. Grey Cloak, your arrival gives me hope, but I don't know if there's much that can be done. Black Frost's army has been growing for ten years. They've overtaken everything. The world is overrun with evil."

"Rhonna was right on most accounts of what she shared with you," Tanlin continued. "Black Frost controls most of the countryside. The underlings have overrun the Wizard Watch. There are more dragons in the sky than ever before. Each and every one of them is a Risker. There are no Sky Riders, no quests to acquire dragon charms. Talon and like groups that served the Wizard Watch have been completely abandoned. Black Frost owns all and rules all."

Grey Cloak's jaw clenched. "He might own the rest of

the world, but he doesn't own us. Now tell me, what happened to the rest of Talon?"

Zora's expression turned bleak. "It's a long story."

"We have all night, and I'm not going anywhere."

"Some are imprisoned, and others disappeared," Tanlin added.

"We're going to find them. We're going to free them." Grey Cloak tapped his index finger on his temple. "Because I have a grand idea."

DID any other members of Talon survive the last ten years?

How will Grey Cloak and Dyphestive defeat the underling threat?

Can the heroes trust Tanlin and Zora, or do they serve a darker master?

Grab your copy of *Dragon Wars: Prisoner Island – Book 9*, On Sale Now! Click here! See pic below.

DON'T FORGET to leave a review for Wizard Watch: Dragon Wars - Book 8. They are a huge help! LINK!

THE FIGURINE OF HEROES: The silver fish is a magical creature that first appeared in *The Darkslayer: Wrath of the Royals – Book 1.*

AND IF YOU haven't already, signup for my newsletter and grab 3 FREE books including the Dragon Wars Prequel. WWW.DRAGONWARSBOOKS.COM

TEACHERS AND STUDENTS, if you would like to order paperback copies for you library or classroom, email craig@thedarkslayer.com to receive a special discount.

GEAR UP in this Dragon Wars body armor enchanted with a +2 Coolness factor/+4 at Gaming Conventions. Sizes range from halfling (Small) to Ogre (XXL). LINK . www.society6.com

ABOUT THE AUTHOR

*Check me out on Bookbub and follow: HalloranOn-BookBub.

*I would love it if you would subscribe to my mailing list: www.craighalloran.com.

*On Facebook, you can find me at The Darkslayer Report or Craig Halloran.

*Twitter, Twitter, Twitter. I am there too: www.twitter.com/CraigHalloran.

*And of course, you can always email me at craig@thedarkslayer.com.

See my book lists below!

ALSO BY CRAIG HALLORAN

Craig Halloran resides with his family outside his hometown of Charleston, West Virginia. When he isn't entertaining mankind, he is seeking adventure, working out, or watching sports. To learn more about him, go to www.thedarkslayer.com.

Check out all my great stories...

Free Books

The Darkslayer: Brutal Beginnings

Nath Dragon—Quest for the Thunderstone

The Chronicles of Dragon Series 1 (10-book series)

The Hero, the Sword and the Dragons (Book 1)

Dragon Bones and Tombstones (Book 2)

Terror at the Temple (Book 3)

Clutch of the Cleric (Book 4)

Hunt for the Hero (Book 5)

Siege at the Settlements (Book 6)

Strife in the Sky (Book 7)

Fight and the Fury (Book 8)

War in the Winds (Book 9)

Finale (Book 10)

Boxset 1-5

Boxset 6-10

Collector's Edition 1-10

Tail of the Dragon, The Chronicles of Dragon, Series 2 (10-book series)

Tail of the Dragon #1

Claws of the Dragon #2

Battle of the Dragon #3

Eyes of the Dragon #4

Flight of the Dragon #5

Trial of the Dragon #6

Judgement of the Dragon #7

Wrath of the Dragon #8

Power of the Dragon #9

Hour of the Dragon #10

Boxset 1-5

Boxset 6-10

Collector's Edition 1-10

The Odyssey of Nath Dragon Series (New Series) (Prequel to Chronicles of Dragon)

Exiled

Enslaved

Deadly

Hunted

Strife

The Darkslayer Series 1 (6-book series)

Wrath of the Royals (Book 1)

Blades in the Night (Book 2)

Underling Revenge (Book 3)

Danger and the Druid (Book 4)

Outrage in the Outlands (Book 5)

Chaos at the Castle (Book 6)

Boxset 1-3

Boxset 4-6

Omnibus 1-6

The Darkslayer: Bish and Bone, Series 2 (10-book series)

Bish and Bone (Book 1)

Black Blood (Book 2)

Red Death (Book 3)

Lethal Liaisons (Book 4)

Torment and Terror (Book 5)

Brigands and Badlands (Book 6)

War in the Wasteland (Book 7)

Slaughter in the Streets (Book 8)

Hunt of the Beast (Book 9)

The Battle for Bone (Book 10)

Boxset 1-5

Boxset 6-10

Bish and Bone Omnibus (Books 1-10)

**CLASH OF HEROES: Nath Dragon meets The Darkslayer
mini series**

Book 1

Book 2

Book 3

The Henchmen Chronicles

The King's Henchmen

The King's Assassin

The King's Prisoner

The King's Conjurer

The King's Enemies

The King's Spies

The Gamma Earth Cycle

Escape from the Dominion

Flight from the Dominion

Prison of the Dominion

The Supernatural Bounty Hunter Files (10-book series)

Smoke Rising: Book 1

I Smell Smoke: Book 2

Where There's Smoke: Book 3

Smoke on the Water: Book 4

Smoke and Mirrors: Book 5

Up in Smoke: Book 6

Smoke Signals: Book 7

Holy Smoke: Book 8

Smoke Happens: Book 9

Smoke Out: Book 10

Boxset 1-5

Boxset 6-10

Collector's Edition 1-10

Zombie Impact Series

Zombie Day Care: Book 1

Zombie Rehab: Book 2

Zombie Warfare: Book 3

Boxset: Books 1-3

OTHER WORKS & NOVELLAS

The Red Citadel and the Sorcerer's Power